UNWRAP HIM

NYLA K.

Copyright © 2022 Nyla K.

All rights reserved.

Paperback ISBN: 979-8-9869189-3-8
eBook ISBN: 979-8-9869189-2-1

Cover Design & Interior Formatting by Cruel Ink Editing & Design

Proofreading by Nice Girl Naughty Edits

Unwrap Him is the intellectual property of Nyla K.

Except permitted under the U.S. Copyright Act of 1976, no part of this publication may be reproduced, distributed, or transmitted in any form or by any means, or stored in a database or retrieval system without prior written permission of the author.

This book is a work of fiction. Any references to historical events, popular culture, corporations, real people, or real places are used fictitiously. Other names, characters, places, and events are products of the author's imagination, and any resemblance to actual events or places or persons living or dead is entirely coincidental.

Dedication

To *Daddies* everywhere.

Blurb

'Twas the night before Christmas...
A secret was looming.
The lust in my heart had become too consuming.
Make no mistake, no blood do we share,
But my guardian was the man whose cross I did bear.
With his icy coal eyes, and peppermint lips,
Under mistletoe I stood, no chance to resist.
For it was on none other than this cold silent night,
That I gave into wrong, and it felt *so damn right*.

Foreword

Ho ho... hoe ;)

This story was originally published as part of the *Twisted Christmas Anthology*, and is now its own novella! Everything from the anthology is here in this book, including a few new chapters; an extended ending for the growly James and his little baker, Jesse.

Please note before reading that this is a taboo story. While the characters are not blood-related, they are family. James has raised Jesse since he was two years old; he's his legal guardian. It contains an age gap, but nothing occurs between them until Jesse is eighteen. There is also mention of death and grief. If things like this make you uncomfortable, I suggest either skipping this story, or proceeding with caution.

Unwrap Him is a super steamy, low-angst novella, perfect for the holiday season, or any time you're looking for smutty, forbidden fun!

Sit back on the couch, grab some hot cocoa and a gingerbread dong, and enjoy!

Content warnings for all Nyla K books can be found here:
www.authornylak.com/content-warnings

ONE
James

"You're breaking up with me??"

My eyes are wide. I can feel them, bugging out of my head like one of those rubber stress-reliever toys.

Leslie sits at the table across from me, arms folded, appearing particularly stone-faced. I can't tell if she's pissed that I'm actually *shocked* at her ending our relationship, or if she's just pissed at me in general.

"Because I can't come home with you for Christmas..." I mutter to fill the silence, blinking over my rounded eyes.

"No, James. Not because you *can't* come home with me for Christmas." She glares at me. "Because you *won't*. There's a big difference."

"I can't leave Jesse—"

"There's that word again!" She snaps, then glances around the cafe we're sitting in to ensure no one's looking. The place is practically empty. "You damn well *can*... if you wanted to. He's eighteen. He'll be fine."

I rake my fingers through my hair. "That's not the point. I'm not going to leave him alone for Christmas. I'm the only family he has."

Leslie keeps her lips zipped, brows furrowing in a petulant scowl that boils my blood just a tad.

"It's not like you even invited him to come along..." I mumble, knowing full well it's a stupid argument.

Jesse wouldn't have wanted to come along.

"Therein lies yet another problem, James," she sighs. "We've been together for two years and I barely know your... son. He obviously doesn't like me. We never spend any time together... I mean, you don't even let me stay over your house. It's like you're purposely keeping me away from him."

"That's not true..."

"It is." She grips the table in frustration, leaning in to whisper-shout at me. "I wanted you to finally meet my parents. I was hoping this would give us a push in the right direction. But as expected, you want no part of it. You're not interested in taking our relationship to the next level, and you're sure as shit not interested in welcoming me into your two-person family." She sits back, gathering her purse. "So we're done."

"Les, just hear me out," I stammer, my thoughts clouding up with what I think I should say. Anything I could do to fix this... Within reason, of course.

"No more excuses, James." She stands. "We're finished. Merry Christmas."

And then she leaves.

She walks right the fuck out of the cafe, leaving me sitting alone at a table, staring at the lipstick on her coffee cup.

I'm not sure why I'm surprised. Things with Leslie have never really felt permanent, which clearly doesn't work for a woman in her thirties who just wasted two years on a man she maybe should have sensed was unlikely to commit.

Leslie was the first person I've been serious with since high school. I suppose I'm what you would call a *chronic bachelor*. I've dated girls, but my default setting is to keep it casual.

Thinking about settling down has always caused some significant discomfort in my gut.

Relationships just aren't at the forefront of my mind. My focus remains on building my business and providing a stable home environment for my kid.

Honestly, Leslie's not wrong in her grievances. I have a tendency to keep Jesse in a bubble. Maybe it's because I'm so afraid of him getting hurt, or attached. But then those things don't seem to satisfy my inner turmoil...

The fact is that eighteen years ago, I made a promise to my best friends in the entire world. At the time, I never imagined I'd have to fulfill that promise... But here we are.

And if a relationship has the potential to in any way compromise my ability to protect Jesse, then I'd rather just avoid the notion altogether.

Twenty minutes of aggrieved simmering later, I pick myself up, dust myself off, and leave the damn cafe. But not without first buying Jesse one of the cake pops he likes. I decide to go back to work for a couple of hours and wrap some things up, since I'll be out of the office for a few days. Christmas, and all.

In my SUV, the radio is on, but I'm too deep in my thoughts to recognize the holiday tunes mumbling in the background. The streets are covered in white after the fresh coat we got last night. According to the weather forecast, Maine will be having a *very* white Christmas this year. It's supposed to keep snowing tonight, and all throughout the holiday.

My vehicle is good in the snow—pretty much a requirement when you live in the Northeast—but the occasional slips of even my all-wheel drive bring back memories...

Of the night my life changed forever.

Pushing it away, I pull up to my building, parking right by the front door. I trudge through the snow in my black boots, slinking inside and closing the door behind me, reveling in the warmth, a stark contrast to the twenty-degree temperatures outside.

Wandering through the reception area, I push open the double-doors, immediately hit with a new wave of heat, and the pungent scent of the grow. We're in between harvests at the moment, which gives us some downtime for the holiday. But it's always balmy as hell in here because... *ya know*. The plants need warmth. At all times.

I own a licensed marijuana grow facility, right here in my hometown of Winthrop. The business took off a few years ago, shortly after it was legalized, and it's been providing me with a steady stream of income ever since. It's still a pretty small setup, but only because I like it that way. I keep my operations to a tight-knit group of employees I trust, and truthfully, I have no desire to expand, though I'm sure I could.

I've known the guys who work for me since high school. I grew up in this town, for the most part, and now I own a business here, and I live here. I guess that makes me a *townie*, though I kind of resent that sort of label because I'm not the guy who walks into a bar like *Cheers*, where everyone knows my name. Maybe they do, but I'd prefer not to be greeted that way.

I keep to myself.

Puttering around the facility, I check on orders, talk with the guys who are still here, and make sure we're all set to be closed for days. It's entirely unnecessary for me to even be here right now, but I guess I'm trying to distract myself.

For as much as I always sort of knew things with Leslie wouldn't stick, getting dumped still sucks. It's a shot to the ego for sure, and yet another reminder that I'm sailing through my thirties with no hope of doing the *normal* thing and starting a family.

But the more interesting part is how secretly relieved I am by that fact.

My life isn't normal. It hasn't been since I was nineteen and I inherited a two-year-old.

Checking my watch, I find that it's after five in the evening. Everyone's itching to go home, which is what I should be doing, too; heading back to our quiet little house to spend yet another Christmas with the only person I have to worry about in this world.

Back in the car and driving slowly over the icy roads, I think about my parents. I don't think about them often, but the holidays usually bring about these kinds of musings.

An only child to two dope fiends, I emancipated myself legally at seventeen. After that, my friends became my family, and the two best ones I had were Trent and Himla. We grew up together, basically inseparable, in similar familial situations. Which is why when Himla became pregnant, it was never a question as to who would be the baby's godfather.

Unfortunately, I never anticipated it being a job I'd have to take on only two years later.

I still remember the night I got the call...

Fear crawls up my spine as the sounds of my own cries fill my memories. The shaking in my hands as I held a frightened two-year-old Jesse, whispering to him that everything would be okay, though I was severely unsure of those promises myself.

It's something you can never prepare for... A loss and an unexpected gift all in one tragic night.

That's what Leslie doesn't understand. It could never be a choice.

When it comes to Jesse, nothing else matters.

TWO
Jesse

I'M PLACING A RED BOW ON THE GIFT BOX WHEN I HEAR the front door slam.

Scrambling, I stuff it underneath the Christmas tree just in time as James shuffles around the corner. I use my body to block the wrapping paper on the floor, not that it really matters. People wrap gifts before Christmas. It's nothing shocking.

He stomps up to me with his arm thrust out, a small paper bag clutched in his grip. I accept it graciously, though the waves of tension radiating from him don't feel very Christmas-cheery.

"Thanks." I open the bag to peek inside, a grin forming on my lips. *Cake pop. Yum.*

"You eat yet?" He grumbles, not waiting for an answer before he's stalking toward the kitchen.

My brow furrows as I follow him. "It's kind of early..." He glances at me over his shoulder when he reaches the marble island, cocking a brow. "But yea, I did," I continue. "Like five times already."

There's the subtlest quirk to his mouth, though it looks like he's trying to keep it contained.

I have a never-ending appetite, and when I'm on any kind of break from school, it's usually a guarantee that I'll spend half the day stuffing my face. *Thank God for my fierce metabolism, I guess.*

James turns back to whatever it is he's doing, sorting through envelopes, a quiet, broody air about him. It's not unusual. My *father*, for all intents and purposes, isn't a wordy man. He's a strong silent type for sure, and emotions turn him into even more of a statue.

I won't say I don't understand it, because I'm an introvert myself. But no one sulks quite like James McAllister.

And because I'm *me*, my need to fill awkward silences becomes an itch I can't *not* scratch. "So when are you leaving for Boston?"

He stiffens. I can see it most in his hunched shoulders as he mutters, "That's not happening."

My surprise whirls. "What do you mean... You're not going?"

He takes in a long breath, then turns slowly, leaning up against the island. "Leslie and I broke up."

The sudden wave of feels hits me head-on, damn-near knocking me down. "Oh..." My mouth is just hanging open, for many generous seconds, before I follow it up with what I'm hoping comes out as a normal response. "What happened?"

He stares at me for a moment, dark gray eyes locked on mine in a way that makes my fingers twitch. I desperately want to look away, but I can't. I'm stuck.

"She just... wasn't the one," he huffs, his tone final as he spins and saunters away, calling over his shoulder, "I'm gonna grab a shower. We can order pizza later, if you're still hungry."

And then he leaves me, standing like a stumped moron in the kitchen with my mouth agape.

Blinking myself out of it, my body's first human reaction is a secret smile, tugging at my lips uncontrollably. I bite down on the bottom one to keep it in check.

They broke up. My heart is pumping wildly in my chest.

Of course I would never wish unhappiness for my adoptive father. He's the only family I have in this world, and I definitely don't want him to become a grumpy old hermit who never finds love.

But at the same time, after enduring two years of that snobby, pretentious woman, I can't find it in myself to be upset about this news.

James deserves better. *Let's be real here...* Leslie is a bitch. She clearly doesn't like me, and I've never been able to figure out why, since she barely knows me at all. You'd think if you were trying to get serious with someone, you'd at least make an effort to bond with his son. But she hardly ever came around.

Part of me held onto that, knowing that if she were making more of an effort to get to know me, it might've actually worked out between them. I'd been secretly hoping she *wouldn't* try, which she didn't. *Good. Who needs her?*

Not my James. I mean, my *father*...

Ugh.

Shaking it off, I waltz back into the living room, a renewed sense of excitement flooding my limbs. I try to push it away, because it's foolish. I would've been fine spending Christmas alone. I had plans, after all.

Bake enough cookies and cupcakes to fill a small village, then eat my feelings while watching *Elf* on repeat until I passed out from a sugar coma.

I never said it wasn't an entirely pathetic plan.

But now I get to spend my favorite holiday with the only

person who matters to me. The person who makes everything good, who I can sit next to in complete silence for hours and hours and still feel nothing but contentment and comfort.

My... *dad.*

A sickening nausea slinks through my gut any time I think of him that way... Because of my own internal hang-ups I've been trying to stuff down for years.

Let's not do this, Jesse. Lock it the fuck up and throw away the key.

Emotions war inside me as I plop onto the couch and turn on the TV. It's already dark outside, and the only light in the room is coming from the Christmas tree and the fluttering glow of *A Charlie Brown Christmas* on the flatscreen.

I watch the movie, lost in my thoughts for the duration, and I'm trying not to ruminate on it, but James has been upstairs a while.

I can't help but wonder if maybe he wants to talk about it... About the break-up.

They *were* together for two years, after all. Even if I'm choosing to believe he didn't love her, maybe he did. Maybe he's... *upset* that they're done. *Not ecstatic like I am.*

The next movie in the lineup, *Rudolph,* is playing as I hear him finally descend the stairs. I can tell by the noise he's tinkering with the wood stove just around the corner, which is good. I'm wearing sweatpants, a hoodie, and fuzzy socks, but I'm still sort of cold. It's frigid outside, reminding me of all the snow we've been getting.

Which then reminds me of the car accident that took my parents.

I don't actually *remember* it. I was only two. But I definitely have vague memories of my parents' existence, and a strong awareness of it being snuffed out.

I was in the car with them that night...

They died. I lived.

And ever since that horrific night, I've been an orphan. Though not really, because my godfather, their best friend, took me in. He assumed guardianship and raised me. He was only one year older than I am now when he became my adoptive father. What a strange notion that is...

I can't even imagine raising a kid right now. I'm a selfish teenager, and I like it that way. Not that I'm self-centered in any way whatsoever, but I like that I get to focus on myself at this point in my life. Next year, I'll graduate high school and then the world is open and full of possibilities. Though the only path my stupid heart seems to want me to follow is the one leading to him...

Meaning right the fuck here.

I force those thoughts away as James walks into the room and up to the couch where I'm sprawled out. He pushes my legs out of the way so he can sit down, as he normally does. A simple and thoroughly uninteresting action, yet the feel of his hand lingers on the skin of my calf, even through the material of my pants.

My stomach is churning as I pull my knees to my chest, leaning back on the couch and pretending to watch the movie, though my peripheral stays on him. He brings a bottle of beer to his lips and takes a long gulp, mesmerizing me with the sight of his Adam's apple bobbing in his throat, sheeted in two-day-old stubble.

My mouth begins to water, and I close my eyes, tight. This can't be happening. *Still.*

Jesus Christ, what more do I have to do? I've tried it all; prayers, distractions of all shapes and sizes... I even bought some crystals and herbs online, hoping to use them to ward off my impure thoughts. Nothing fucking works.

I'm still hopelessly infatuated with my own goddamn guardian, and it's sick.

Inconvenient and so damn wrong.

What is wrong with me? Am I some kind of pervert?

I came to terms with my sexuality pretty early on. By the time I was twelve, I already knew I liked boys not girls, and it's never been something I've struggled with. Sure, I don't broadcast my sexuality to the world, but that's because I don't broadcast anything. I like keeping to myself. I have friends, and they know I'm gay. I came out to James when I was fourteen, and he didn't even bat an eye. He just told me that he loves and accepts me no matter what.

Why in the fucking world that made me swoon, I have no clue.

And from the moment I came into my own as a teen, growing slowly from a boy into a man, the only person I've managed to develop feelings for is the one I can't have.

The one I *won't* have. Ever.

It sucks balls. And not in the good way.

The movie keeps playing, into the next one, and James orders us pizza. It arrives quick enough and we eat. I indulge in my cake pop afterward while James finishes his second beer, quietly asking me to grab him another one. Taking the empty bottle from him, I jump up and race to the kitchen. He's been asking me to get him beers since I was old enough to carry them, which only serves to remind me that I'm his kid. And I always will be.

I fucking loathe how heavy that fact sits in my gut as I return to the living room with a new bottle.

Sinking onto the couch, I hold out the beer, and when he takes it, our fingers brush. Tell me why that one insignificant touch sends a rack of shivers through my lower stomach and a twitch into my crotch. I have to fight not to roll my eyes at myself.

"Thanks, kid," he murmurs, sipping from the bottle.

Kid. Yea... That's what I am. His fucking son... Forever a child in his eyes.

I barely even notice I'm shivering so hard, teeth chattering, until he grunts, "You want me to start a fire?" He nods toward the fireplace across the living room.

"Uh... no." My voice scrapes, and I clear my throat. "I'm fine."

"Good, 'cause it's actually pretty warm in here," he huffs.

My side-eye takes in the sight of him, watching the TV and ignoring my fidgets. He's wearing jeans and a t-shirt, nowhere near as bundled as I am, and clearly, he's comfortable. The lines of his wide chest, broad shoulders and thick arms are visible beneath the material, prompting me to tug my lower lip between my teeth.

I'm not cold either, James... Actually, I'm burning the fuck up.

Scolding myself internally, I decide to take on a new tactic for distraction, something that's proven effective in the past. Prying into his heavily-guarded armor.

"So what happened with Leslie?" I rest my head on the back of the couch, eyes locked on the television screen.

"Nothing." His deep voice rumbles at my side, giving me even more chills.

"That doesn't sound right," I keep poking. "Two years and it just ends? There's gotta be a reason."

He stays silent for a few lingering moments, swallowing a long pull from the bottle before he finally answers, "I don't think I'm in love with her..."

My stomach clenches. "You don't *think*?"

His eyes shift to mine for a split second. "No. I'm... not. I never have been."

"Why not?"

"What's with the third degree, kid?" He narrows his gaze at me from the side. "You breaking into investigative journalism or something?"

"Uh no." I give him a look. "That would make for a very bland piece of writing. No one cares about your love life."

He lets out a throaty chuckle, one that slithers into my brain through my ears and presses on something that releases a shot of dopamine. James doesn't laugh often, and when he does, and I'm responsible for it, I swear to God, it's like a hit of some really good drugs.

He sighs it out and shakes his head. "I can't be with someone who doesn't accept me for who I am... and who's in my life."

A painful throb of guilt stabs me in the chest like a sharp blade.

Me... They broke up because of me.

It's my fault.

James will die alone because he's too busy fretting over his grown-ass adoptive son, who's secretly never happier than when it's just the two of us.

I'm such a selfish asshole.

Correction, a perverted *selfish asshole.*

There are so many things I want to say, but I won't let myself. Instead, I just slither off the couch and mumble, "I'm going to bed."

Giving him my back, I only make it two steps before I hear him calling. "Jess... Don't be like that. You wanted to know, so I fucking told you."

I peek at him over my shoulder, forcing a smile. "No, I know. I'm just tired."

Leaving the room quickly, while trying to act like I'm feeling totally normal inside, I stumble up the steps into my bedroom. Once inside with the door closed, I take in a long breath, squeezing my eyes shut while releasing it slowly.

I hate everything about what I've become. A thorn in the side of the person I love most in this world. The *only* person I love, for that matter.

I feel like such a moron as I pace around my bedroom. Obsessing over my own father—*figure*—for years, like a total creep. I just want these feelings to go away, but I'm not sure they ever will. It's like a sickness... A terminal disease with no cure.

Trust me, I've tried to transfer the feelings onto others. I've hooked up with a few guys, more in the past year than before. I didn't even have my first kiss until I was fifteen, because I never wanted to give it to anyone who wasn't my own goddamn guardian. But I finally bit the bullet and did it. And it felt... so fucking wrong.

But I kept getting back up on that horse, only to be tossed off every time in disappointment. I lost my virginity six months ago to a dude from school, and even that just felt like a means to an end.

We've fucked a couple of times since, and it's alright I guess, because he's hot. He's the captain of the football team, but he's *straight*, so no one's allowed to know he likes putting his dick in guys. Not that I even care, because I don't want anything from him. Anything but a meaningless distraction.

An ultimate dissatisfaction.

Crawling into my bed beneath the covers, I grab my phone where it's been charging on the nightstand. Speak of the devil, I have a new text from Tanner. I open it to find a dick pic, and I roll my eyes. Why am I not surprised one bit?

It's a decent dick, and I guess it sort of gives my own erection some traction, but not much. I'm too lost in my own head, too focused on my sick crush to even bother responding. Instead, I stuff my phone under the pillow next to me and close my eyes.

My hand slithers down to the waistband of my sweats, slipping inside and grazing myself over my boxers. Teasing my hardening flesh, my mind swims with images of the man downstairs. The man who's almost twice my age, and technically my *father*. Though not by blood, it's still wrong. I've known him literally my entire life. He raised me... Changed my diapers and shit.

It's twisted.

He taught me how to ride a bike, how to shave, how to drive; he comforted me when I got hurt, and scolded me when I fucked up. He's been my fucking *father* my whole life, yet now I look at him like he's supposed to be more than that.

I've always prayed that it's just an attraction. Because he's hot as fuck, nothing more.

But as my lips quiver and my fist curls around my erection to visions of him touching me the way I'm touching myself, I can't even be sure.

All I know is that I'm jerking off to thoughts of my dad right now...

And less than two minutes later, I'm coming in my hand with *his* face in my brain.

THREE
James

It's just after midnight when I drag myself up the steps to my bedroom.

I'm barely even tired, but I just knew if I stayed downstairs on the couch, I'd end up drinking too many beers and passing out down there, which is something I'd prefer not to do.

I don't want to seem like I'm drowning my sorrows, because I'm not. I dodged a bit of a bullet when Leslie ended things. I'm glad it happened, though it pains me to admit it. Why wouldn't I want to get serious with a beautiful woman? It doesn't make much sense.

I just can't stop thinking about how Jesse clammed up when I mentioned the reason for the inevitable end to the relationship. I never meant for him to feel guilty. At the end of the day, it's not his fault at all. I was the one keeping Leslie at a distance. It had nothing to do with him. These are all *my* issues.

Maybe I'm not meant to settle down. With anyone.

Inside my bedroom, I strip down to my boxers and climb into bed. Beneath the covers, I lie on my back, staring at the ceiling for a while, my internal obsessing whisking me away until I barely even remember how I got to where I am in my head.

I'm not a great sleeper. I've always struggled with getting a full eight hours. Or even five. But part of me thinks I run better on a lack of sleep. I'm fine with it.

When I hear sudden footsteps in the hallway, I'm on high alert. My bedroom door is open a crack, done so for a reason. So that he doesn't hurt himself.

Because when he staggers inside, he's shuffling like a zombie, eyelids fluttering as his heavy steps clunk him right into the side of my bed. And then he crashes down onto it, nestling up on top of the covers.

I let out a despondent sigh.

Jesse sleepwalks. He's been doing it since he was a kid, and we've never been able to get to the root of the problem. The first few times were terrifying. I'd wake up in the morning and find him on the bathroom floor, or curled up in a ball in the hallway. Thankfully he's never injured himself, but that's why I put up a gate at the top of the stairs, just in case. He seems to walk just fine in his sleep, making it all the way downstairs in the past. But it's not a risk I'm willing to take. The last thing I want is him tripping down the steps and breaking his neck.

He's seen a therapist before, where he was diagnosed with some mild anxiety. They gave him sleeping pills in an attempt to keep him thoroughly conked out, but he doesn't like taking them. Says they make him groggy.

So instead, we got the gate, and confined him to upstairs. And now, his subconscious brings him in only one direction. My bedroom.

I know it's not healthy. I'm not a lunatic. But the thing is, I don't have the heart to stop him. Jesse is a strong-willed kid. He's smart and grounded, but he's always suffered within himself. He's quiet about his emotions, and he internalizes everything. I think I know where he gets it from...

For as much as I've raised him, as well as I could as a nineteen-year-old without a clue, I know Jesse feels the absence of his real parents. He'd never voice it to me, but he does. He knows I'm not them... And I've always wondered if I'm glad about that fact or saddened by it.

I don't know if I want to be his father, or just his guardian. There's a big difference in the two.

Sure, I've done everything I can to give him a loving, stable home over the years. He doesn't call me *Dad*, and I'm totally fine with that. I try to talk about his parents with him as much as possible, but at this point, it's been so long since they were around, I barely remember what they were like anymore.

It fucking sucks. Because they were my only family...

And now I have this boy of theirs, who's supposed to be mine just as much, and I don't have any way of helping him. I don't think he's broken on the inside... I sure as shit hope not, because I've spent my entire adult life trying to make sure he's whole.

Jesse turns in the bed, shifting onto his stomach with his face mashed into the pillow. My bed is big enough that there's plenty of room between us. I wouldn't let this happen if there weren't. But I also don't make any immediate attempts at moving him, and I don't really know why.

I just want to keep him comfortable for a little while longer, and if this will do it, then fine. I'm not sure why he comes into my room in his sleep, but I refuse to make him feel bad about it, or myself either, for that matter. I don't know if he remembers any part of doing this, but we don't talk about it.

And let's just say, this is one giant reason why I always spent the night at Leslie's house. Over two years of seeing each other, she'd only spent the night in my bed twice. And both times, I locked my bedroom door, and stayed awake all night, stressing about Jesse, hoping he wouldn't try to get in while she was here.

Fucked up, I know, but what can I do?

I'm better off alone. Again, because if the alternative is alienating Jesse, well then, it's just not going to happen.

The sounds of Jesse's soft breaths begin to lull me into a sleepy trance, and I force myself out of it. I'm going to have to move him soon, meaning I absolutely cannot fall asleep. If he wakes up in my bed, it would be the most confusing, awkward thing ever, and we can't have that.

Rolling onto my side, I observe him for a moment. His light blonde hair looks almost platinum in this light, mussed up and strewn about. Such a unique color. He definitely got it from Himla.

His mother was of Swedish origin, and while Trent had a slightly darker complexion and hair, Jesse came out as a spitting image of his mom. The pale skin, hair a color that people choose from bottles, and those golden eyes, like wildflower honey.

He's a real looker, the kid. Whoever he ends up with will be one lucky son-of-a-bitch.

He's wearing the same thing he was when he went to bed; high school football team hoodie with the torn front pocket, gray sweatpants, and some ridiculous fuzzy *Rick And Morty* socks he wears constantly. It brings a curl to my lips, promptly falling away when I recall him storming out of the room at barely eight o'clock. Jesse doesn't typically go to bed early either, so I just know he was upset about what I told him... Thinking he was the reason for Leslie and I ending things.

I don't want him to worry about me. He doesn't need that stress. I'll be fine. All I have to do is be here for him.

Fuck love anyway, right?

All relationships are doomed to fail before they even start.

The next time I glance at the clock on my nightstand, I

notice that it's almost three in the morning. *Where the hell did the time go?*

Sliding out of bed as gently as possible, I round to his side, bending down and scooping him up into my arms.

Jesse's not a small kind by any means. He's just under six feet, one-hundred-and-seventy pounds of slim muscle. Yet when he's sleeping, it's so easy for me to hoist him up and carry him to his bedroom, just like when he was little.

His calm breaths tickle the flesh of my neck as I bring him across the hall, back into his bedroom. Laying him down on the bed, I pull the covers over his waist, giving him one last lingering glance as he lets out a purr, stretching before nestling up beneath his comforter, still lost in his slumber.

Unsure of what drives me to it, I reach down and brush my fingers through his silky blonde locks, pushing the strands of ivory from where they want to flop over his forehead. It reminds me of the times I put him to bed as a child. That's the thought resting at the front of my mind as I leave his bedroom and go back to my own.

Crawling back into bed, I lie on my side, facing the empty spot.

And I don't fall asleep until the pale glow of sunrise peeks through the window.

FOUR
Jesse

My eyes creep open to sunlight streaming in through the partially drawn curtains of my bedroom window. Groggily, I blink myself awake, feeling around the bed.

Something feels *off*, and I know what that means...

I may have walked in my sleep.

I know I do it. I've suffered from sleepwalking for years. Back when it started, it was nerve-racking, waking up not in my bed. James took me to a doctor a few times, but nothing has really helped. I accepted it long ago. And though I have no recollection of what I do, wandering around at night unconscious, I always have this feeling when I wake up knowing I've done it. Like a dream I can't quite grasp.

These recollections resonate in my mind... It's been this way for a long time. And now I can barely even tell where my dreams end and reality begins.

But I haven't woken up outside of my bed in years. Somehow, I always seem to find my way back, which is interesting, to say the least.

Rubbing my eyes, I fling my legs out of bed, cringing at how bright it is outside. The sun is reflecting off the snow, blinding me even through the curtains. I make my way into the bathroom to brush my teeth and take a shower.

Once I'm done and dressed in black jeans and a flannel, I head downstairs, the smell of bacon and eggs rumbling my stomach. I swing into the kitchen, where James is standing in front of the stove, poking at things with a spatula.

Pushing away the awkwardness I always feel around him lately, I chirp, "Good morning."

He does a little nod over his shoulder, nothing but a grunt for a response. Pretty on-brand for my adoptive father.

Pulling out a chair, I take a seat at the island, watching him intently. I do most of the cooking in our household, because I love it. Cooking is my favorite thing, baking in particular, and I love trying out new recipes on my guardian. I get no protest whatsoever from James, since he loves to eat, same as me. We have powerful appetites between the two of us.

But if it were left up to James, we'd eat bacon and eggs for every meal, because it's pretty much all he can cook. Maybe that's part of the reason I learned so young. I wanted to make sure he got a proper meal. And myself, too... But I guess I just enjoy doting on him.

My jaw tenses, reminding myself for the millionth time that it's strictly familial. Nothing more.

The room is devoid of conversation. The only sounds are those of the food cooking and James cleaning up as he goes. When he's done, he brings over two plates, setting one down in front of me, then taking a seat himself across the island with his own, immediately digging in.

We eat in silence, as usual. James isn't a big talker. He

never has been. If I want his words, I need to drag them out of him. Kind of like last night, though I have no desire to bring up the relationship topic again.

James finishes his food first and stays seated at the table until I'm done. We're not a typical family in any real way, but we do have our traditions. Like eating together, for one. James has insisted, since I was a child, that we always sit down for our meals together, when we're both here. Regardless of whether we do it in silence, apparently having this family time is important.

Speaking of traditions… "So we're watching *A Christmas Story* tonight, right?" I ask him, glancing up while nibbling my last bite of bacon.

His lips quirk in a casually placating way. "Wouldn't miss it for the world."

My stomach does a weird hop thing I ignore as I stand up and bring our plates to the sink. I also tend to do most of the cleaning and housework, just because James works hard, and I like for him to come home to a clean house.

And yes, I realize the more I reveal with this inner monologue, the more I sound like a housewife. I swear to God, I'm not trying to be this way. It's just what I do.

As much as I say James is a loner, I'm sort of the same. I have a few friends I hang out with on weekends, or occasionally after school. But I've never even needed a curfew because I just… love coming home.

I like spending time here, alone… or with him. I probably sound like the ultimate hermit too, but I can't find it in myself to care. I've spent my teen years going to school and getting good grades. I've taken a few culinary classes, and I think if I were to go to college, it would definitely be for baking. But I'm eighteen and I haven't even applied to school. At the very least, I'm taking a year. Just to figure myself out, I guess.

To see if I'm even capable of cutting the cord and leaving James. Honestly, I fucking hate the idea.

The thing about my adoptive father is that he doesn't push. I'd like to think he does so because he wants me around, too. But the more likely reason is that he's not that kind of dad. He's told me before that he raised me the way he thought my parents would have.

It makes me happy and wrenches my gut at the same time.

Busying myself with the dishes, I ignore how hyperaware I always seem to be of his presence in the room. It's like I can feel him when he's close, and I miss the feeling when he's not. *I'm a fucking whacko. I need to get a grip.*

Prime example being how when his thumping footsteps move in closer to where I'm standing, my back goes rigid.

"Going outside to gather more firewood," he says, his brogue assaulting my back, so startling in its nearing vibrations, I actually flinch. He places his coffee mug in the sink, arm brushing mine as he does. I have goosebumps. I can fucking *see* them. "It's supposed to start snowing more in a couple hours."

"Mhm, okay." My voice sounds annoyingly breathy as I scrub the same spot on the pan I've been doing for minutes now.

James is still standing right the fuck next to me, and I can *feel* him staring at the side of my face. I'd love to turn and see what he wants, but I just know I don't possess the means to do so normally. If I look at him right now, I fear he'll be able to see all the sickening perversions living in my brain.

So I just keep washing as he finally slinks past me toward the back door, his scent lingering in the air even after he's gone.

It's mouthwatering. Masculine and heady, like hemp and citrus and fire. I've been smelling it my whole life, and now it's my favorite smell.

Ugh. Someone call the shrink.

That's probably the other reason I stopped going to therapy. I was always terrified that I'd accidentally blurt out something alluding to my hidden ravenous crush on my guardian. And I can't have that. No one can know.

It's my dirty, shameful secret.

As I finish up the dishes, my gaze lifts to the window above the sink. James is outside, carrying wood from the shed and piling it up on the back deck. I can't see the deck from right here, but I already know that's what he's doing. From here, I can only see him when he trudges through the snow to the shed in his big work boots, deep chocolate brown suede coat, gloves on his hands, and a hat I bought him for Christmas last year resting atop his mane of dark, shaggy hair.

I bite my lip, hands washing on auto-pilot while I'm swept up in yet another trance watching him. The hair on his angled jaw and down his throat is growing out. I *love* it. He's fuckhot in many ways, but none more than with a few days of stubble turning into a barely-beard. It looks rough and rugged...

Imagine how it must feel on bare skin...

Blinking hard, I shake myself out of it as best I can. But it doesn't quite work, and I'm still staring at him... Hauling a pile of wood in his arms like a sexy Paul Bunyan, muscles surely constricting beneath all his layers of clothes. It's freezing outside, but he might be sweating a little from the exertion...

The cut up lines in his chest and abs dewy and glistening.

I swallow down a soft moan that wants to erupt from my throat as my cock swells in my jeans.

And then a sharp slice of pain tugs me back to reality when I realize I just cut myself on a knife in the sink.

"Fucking bitch..." I grumble, *at* myself maybe more than *to* myself. Because I'm sitting here ogling my goddamn father, and not paying attention to what I'm doing.

It's not that deep a cut, but still, droplets of blood fall into the soapy water in the sink. Bringing my finger to my mouth, I suck it for a second while grabbing a paper towel to wrap around my wound of stupidity.

"You're a moron," I whisper, shaking my head while applying pressure to the cut.

I shut the water off in the sink just as the back door flings open, the large form stomping in, bringing the cold air with him for only a brief second before he slams the door.

He takes one look at me and his brow furrows. "What happened?"

"Um, nothing," I stutter, face shimmying back and forth. He cocks his head and lifts an eyebrow like he doesn't believe me. It's his trademark look. "Just a little cut," I sigh. "No big deal."

James drops the logs in his arms over by the wood stove, then stalks up to me while sliding off his gloves, not waiting for me to consent before he grabs my hand. He removes the paper towel to check out the cut.

"It's not too deep." His gray eyes lift to mine. "Does it hurt?"

I have no voice. I wouldn't even know what words to use if I could produce some, because he's standing so damn close to me, holding my hand. His are freezing, but I think the chills I'm getting aren't necessarily from that.

God, if I thought his scent was powerful before, now, it's getting me high, as are the tingles charging through his skin directly into mine.

My head shakes subtly; *stupidly*, like a deer in headlights who's trying to answer a question for some reason before he gets run the fuck over by a big sexy Mack truck.

James eyes me for a moment, obviously not picking up on any of the tension that's completely one-sided. It's good that he can't tell I'm fumbling and my dick is two seconds from becoming visible in my pants. But it also makes me feel like even more of a sick, perverted loser, lusting after someone who so clearly would never even consider the majorly fucked up shit that goes through my mind on almost a minute-ly basis.

"Keep the pressure on it," he says firmly, giving me my hand back as he stomps across the room.

I already know he's going for the First-Aid kit, which is what I should be doing on my own. I'm eighteen goddamn years old. I'm not four. I don't need him to kiss my boo-boos.

But then... That might make it better.

Ew, shut up, you fool.

James comes back with a Band-Aid and some antiseptic ointment. He dresses my cut, and when he's done, he actually gives me a rare, pleased smile.

My heart is jumping like a complete psycho in my chest.

Until he rasps, "Good as new," and taps me on the chin with his knuckles, before stalking away, back to his wood.

Jesus...

Absentmindedly, I run my thumb over the Band-Aid on my index finger. *You're his kid. His fucking son.*

Cleanse the creepy, Jess.

FIVE
James

Snow is falling outside. Again.

It's been coming down for hours. I've already shoveled the driveway once, but at this point, I figure it's Christmas Eve.

Time to relax.

Jesse and I just finished dinner. He made lamb chops with roasted potatoes, squash, and salad. It was fucking amazing.

The kid can cook. Seriously, it's like a God-given talent he also happens to work really hard at. I know it's his favorite hobby, and also something he'd like to make into a career one day. And I just want to be supportive of that, because it's a smart, achievable goal.

When Jesse told me he wanted to take a year off after graduation to figure out his next steps, I was on board. I know some parents might look at college as the only direction after high school, but I respectfully disagree. I never went to college, though I did take an online business course, which was tremendously helpful. But I just don't think everyone needs to go into staggering debt for a piece of paper you hang on your wall.

In some professions, sure. It's necessary. But Jesse could

easily work his way up in restaurants and then maybe open his own someday without a college degree.

Regardless of all that, though, I just want to support him. In whatever he chooses to do with his life. And if that choice happens to keep him at home for at least a little while longer, well then... great.

Because not that I'd ever admit it out loud to anyone, but I don't want to think about what my life would look like without the kid here.

I'm not sure I even know who I am without Jesse...

A business owner, yes. A friend? Maybe, to a couple of guys who still put up with me. Other than that, though, I'm a father to an eighteen-year-old, and that's a huge part of my personality. If Jesse leaves, he takes a significant chunk of me with him.

The thought is all too real, so I stuff it away and grab a couple of glasses. It's eight at night, and our tradition is about to start.

Every Christmas Eve, we light up the fireplace and drink eggnog while watching *A Christmas Story*. We've been doing it since Jesse was old enough to hold a cup. It's not a lively or exciting event, but it's ours and I enjoy it.

If I had gone with Leslie, I would've missed out on our tradition for the first time in ever...

No, that's unacceptable. It never would have worked.

Although we were together for two years, Leslie never spent Christmas with me. And I can't for the life of me picture her here now, snuggling up on the couch next to us with a cup of eggnog. She doesn't even consume dairy.

I roll my eyes while pouring eggnog into each glass. Truthfully, I can't picture *anyone* else on that couch. Except maybe Trent and Himla. But even so, the memories I have of them are so distorted now, that picture doesn't quite fit either.

It's just Jesse and me. The two of us against the world.

Reaching up into the cupboard, I grab the bottle of brandy, pouring some into my eggnog. Then I pause, taking only a couple of seconds to consider it before I add some to Jesse's glass, too.

He's eighteen, after all. I'm sure he's drank before. Hell, I gave him a beer once or twice.

It's Christmas Eve and this can be a new addition to our tradition, now that he's a man.

The thought warms my gut as I bring our drinks into the living room. Jesse is already nestled up on his side of the couch, feet buried in his Christmas *Rick And Morty* socks this time, resting on the couch cushion. The kid always takes up the entire couch, which isn't very big as it is.

Waltzing over, I plop down, sitting on his toes.

"Rude," he huffs, pulling his feet back, though there's a visible grin sneaking out with the word.

Handing him a glass, he takes it, holding it up for a toast.

"Merry Christmas Eve, kid," I tell him, clinking on his glass.

We both sip at the same time, my eyes going to the movie, which has just started. But the sound of Jesse gurgling brings my gaze back to him.

"What the hell is in this?" His face scrunches.

It reminds me of when he was little and he tried liver for the first time. *Let's just say that's one protein that has stayed far off the menu since.*

"Little brandy in the nog never hurt anyone." I smirk at him. "It'll put some hair on your chest."

"I don't need hair on my chest," he grumbles. "I have it everywhere else."

A laugh bubbles from my throat. "Congratulations."

He continues smothering a smile, taking another sip from

the glass. "This is actually really good." His cheeks are growing pink already. "Strong."

Grinning, I turn back to the movie, resting my head on the back of the couch. "Take it slow, killa. I don't want you getting sick."

"I'm sure I can handle a little brandy," he mumbles, and when my eyes flit to him once more, half the glass is gone.

Narrowing my gaze, it's occurring to me that Jesse is usually the forthcoming one of the two of us. He's the one who tells me what's going on with him, and he's also the one who drags information out of me. I'm a closed book, but Jesse isn't like that. He enjoys sharing, and now I feel like kind of an asshole for never asking him stuff.

It also makes me wonder about the things he hasn't been as open about...

"You know, if you drink at parties, you can tell me." I go for casual with my tone, focusing on the TV screen while I watch him in my peripheral. "I wouldn't be mad. I mean, how could I? I did the same thing at your age."

A year before I became a father, and grew up eye-blink fast.

"I've had a few drinks before." He shrugs, innocently enough, and I know he's not lying. Jesse's a terrible liar, so he rarely does it. At least, not to me. "Usually just beer. Maybe a shot or two. But I'm not one of those kids who likes to get shit-faced at parties and embarrass myself."

I nod along. It makes sense. I was the same way when I was young. Latent insecurities make it hard enough to socialize, especially when you're worried the whole time that people are mocking you behind your back. I'd rather keep a clear head. And I realize that sounds strange coming from someone who grows marijuana for a living. But I really just like the plants. I rarely smoke it myself.

Growing things has always been a passion of mine.

"I get that," I tell him. "You want to stay cognizant." My mind begins to drift... "Like if you're on a date or something..."

His eyes fling to mine, rounding as they do. The shine in the gold of his irises tells me he might be getting a little buzz already.

"Guys at parties can't be trusted," I add.

"I'm not... I don't..." His voice stammers and he clears his throat. "I don't date guys at parties."

"Do you date at all?" I ask, suddenly curious, because we've literally never talked about him dating before. He's never brought anyone home, or told me anything about his love life.

The flush in his face is much more prominent now. "Um... not... much?" He says it like he's asking me, which curves my lips.

"You're still interested in guys though, right?" I keep pushing, mainly because now his awkwardness is entertaining to me. "Or have you added girls to the mix?"

He shifts in his seat while I try to contain my evil chuckles. "No. I only like men." His brows zip together as he stutters, "Boys... *Guys*." He lifts the glass to his mouth and chugs the rest of his drink.

Pressing my lips together, I force myself not to react. *He's dying right now, and it's pretty adorable.*

"Okay, just double-checking," I sigh through a grin. "You don't talk to me about this stuff, so..."

"You don't talk to me about your relationships," he bites back, finger tapping on his empty glass.

I sip my own slowly. "Well, aside from Leslie it's not a very thrilling story. Not that she was *exciting* either."

"Why were you with her, then?" He mumbles his question, and when my eyes dart to his, they widen in remorse. "I'm sorry..."

"No, it's a valid question." I blink, pausing for a moment

while considering my words. "I guess I was just... waiting to see."

"To see what?" His voice is quietly curious. As if he's intrigued.

My shoulders slump. "If I could end up loving her."

We're both quiet this time, for at least a full minute, before he asks, "But you didn't?"

I shake my head, solemnly, though I'm not exactly upset about this fact. I think it just means I might never fall in love... with anyone.

I finish my drink while we watch the movie in silence, the only sounds in the room from the TV and the crackling fire.

"That was good," Jesse speaks after a while, and I glance over to see him holding up his glass. "Can I have more?"

I shrug and stand. "Why the hell not."

Taking both of our empty cups to the kitchen, I pour more eggnog, and even more brandy this time. I'm not trying to get drunk, and I'm definitely not trying to get Jesse drunk either, even though I'm now fairly certain this amount of alcohol could get him there, since apparently he's not a big drinker. I'm pleased by this fact. I like that he has a good head on his shoulders and knows that drowning your sorrows in vices is never the way.

But I also think I like this new part of our tradition. Opening him up a bit is a good thing. I'd like to know more about his life, and I want him to feel comfortable sharing.

Back in the living room, I hand him his fresh drink and plop down on his toes again. But rather than pulling them away this time, he wiggles them under my thigh.

I can feel my grin, but I squash it, and mutter, "Are you cold?"

He shakes his head. "No. Just... getting cozy."

I keep my face aimed forward at the television, feeling him

relax, leaning back and wedging his feet further beneath my legs. I'm sort of tense, and I'm not sure why, so I ignore it and focus on the movie.

But for some reason, I'm abnormally *aware* of Jesse while he sips his drink. It's as if I can feel his buzz as he melts deeper into the couch.

Then it dawns on me that I might be getting a buzz on myself, which is why I'm feeling this way.

Who knows.

The movie continues, and we watch as we always do. Chuckling at certain parts we know so well. By the time the kid on the screen is getting his tongue stuck to the pole, I'm so relaxed I barely even notice that Jesse's feet aren't under my legs anymore. They're resting on my lap.

He has his legs draped over mine. *When did that happen?*

We've never sat like this before, and for some reason, it's keying me up once again. I'm not sure why. It's not unusual for him to sprawl out and take up the whole couch. It's kind of his thing. But his long legs stretched over my thighs seem to be the only things I can pay any attention to, for minutes on end.

I'm acting like I'm watching the movie, but really my eyes keep falling to his feet in those cartoon socks, toes visibly wiggling every now and then.

It's good. He's happy. He's comfortable... That's all I care about.

Not my own bizarre anxiety, which doesn't make any sense.

The night wears on. The movie ends and starts up again, on a loop, because that's another part of the tradition, for everyone apparently, not just us.

I'm lulled into an easy state, my hands resting on Jesse's shins once the drink is long empty, cup down on the floor. After a while, my eyelids begin to flutter, sleepiness overtaking me.

The last thing I remember is glancing at Jesse, to find him out cold, head lolling off to the side, his chest rising and falling in content breaths of slumber.

A soft smile graces my lips, and I lean back, succumbing to the sleep that steals me.

Warmth.

All I can feel is warm, everywhere.

A heat I didn't have before has settled over my skin, something like a dream burning me right up.

Tightness clutches, and it takes several generous moments for me to realize it's spreading from my gut up to my chest.

Starting in my loins.

Foggy and lost in my subconscious, a fantastic sensation washes over me. Tingles sweep through my limbs, settling below my waist.

Sex.

That's what it feels like. A sex dream.

Lying back, I give in to the pleasure, my cock firm and my balls aching. It feels so fucking good, there's no way this is real. I haven't had something this nice in a while.

My eyes aren't open, and I'm certain I'm deep in my own peaceful dreamland, the familiar warm wetness sliding up and down my dick. It only takes me another moment of fizzling desire to recognize it as a mouth.

I'm getting head in my dream. *Awesome.*

The tongue cradles my erection, stiff and pumped full of blood, soft lips and saliva coating me, sucking and sucking, at such a leisurely pace, it's almost as if it's barely happening at all. The mouth is just holding my cock, taking its time, and it feels divine.

Leslie? I want to ask, because who else would have my dick in their mouth?

But that assumption doesn't feel accurate. It feels... different. Unlike anything Leslie did to me in our two years together.

So it must be a mystery woman, then. Sucking me off in my dream like a good little slut, taking me all the way back until my head nudges her throat.

"So good..." I whimper, dazed and enraptured by a thick cloud of arousal.

My hips flick, gradually, with the movements of the mouth, feeding my length between the softest lips ever created. That's how I know it's not real. No one has lips this plush. Like pillows of silk, working up and down my dick so slowly, it's driving me insane.

"You teasing me, baby...?" My sleepy words fall out on an exhale of calm breath, fingers twitching at my sides with the need to hold her face and guide her.

Suck me like a good girl...

Inching one hand upward, my fingers dance along a sharp jaw. But I don't even notice.

Not until I reach hair. Smooth, silky strands fill my fingers. But it's short.

It's too short. There's not much of it at all.

That's weird. Do I know any girls with short hair like this...?

I'm distracted by my confusion when the tongue swirls around the crown of my cock, dragging a quiet moan from my throat. My hips shift, pushing between those luscious lips once more.

This feels so real. More real than any dream I've had before.

My mind finally awakens enough for my eyes to creep open.

And I freeze.

My heart stops cold from its steady thump.

Now I'm certain I'm dreaming. Because it looks like... *Jesse*.

Jesse with his eyes closed, lying on his stomach between my parted thighs. With my dick in his mouth.

This isn't real. There's no fucking way.

It's a dream. It has to be.

More like an aching nightmare.

SIX
Jesse

The throb in my balls is what wakes me up.

They're pumping so strong, it's as if my heart is between my legs.

That and I think I'm drooling in my sleep. I can feel saliva trickling from the corner of my mouth, and my jaw is sore.

I must have been grinding my teeth.

But as I slip back into reality from wherever I was nestled in my subconscious, I find myself... sucking on something.

My first realization is that I must have been sleepwalking. I fell asleep on the couch next to James, watching the movie. I was curled up on my side, dozing.

But now I'm on my stomach, and without even noticing it until right now, my hips are grinding into the cushion.

I register my dick, stiff as a metal pole, trying to jam its way through my pants and into the fabric of the couch. My hips are doing its bidding, driving in slow thrusts as I hump and hump.

But the more I come to, the more I taste... salt. And skin.

That's what wakes me fully the fuck up. The fact that I have something hard in my mouth, and I'm sucking on it, and it tastes suspiciously like a dick.

My eyelids flutter, and I glance up. Terror seizes my entire body.

James is lying before me, beneath me, sort of. His legs parted with me in between, pants unbuttoned and open. Dick out.

In my mouth.

His dick is in my mouth.

Holy fuck. Oh my God.

No no no... what am I doing?? How is this happening??

Panic sweeps through me fast, but I'm too frozen to move. I close my eyes and will myself back into the dream.

That's gotta be it, right? I'm dreaming.

There's no earthly way this is happening for real.

Opening my eyes a crack, I peek back up. And I catch the tail-end of James's deep gray gaze, locked on mine. Before his lids slam shut.

Confusion ripples in my mind. *Does he know what's happening? Is he awake?*

No. No one's awake, because this is a dream. It's not real.

And my attention is immediately back on the fact that I still have his dick in my mouth.

It's long, so *so* long, and thick. Huge, really.

That must be why my jaw is sore...

My tongue slides on its own, no clue why, but it does. And a sound graces my ears.

A hum. A soft, raspy noise that came straight from the chest of a grown-ass man.

It sounds like him.

I can't deny the fact that I'm clearly in love with this. If it is a dream, it's the best one ever. And it has to be one, which is why I'm not moving my mouth away, nor is he stopping me.

It's not really happening... And in my dreams, I get to do the things I could never do in real life.

Like sucking off my father.

Cringing, I dispel that thought. *He's not my father...*

Yea, so he raised me. Big deal. Right *now*, he's just the hot as fuck dude in his thirties who's letting me wrap my lips around his severely impressive erection.

My cock jolts beneath me, precum dripping from my tip. I can feel it, and judging by the stickiness in my boxers, that wasn't the first time.

Goddamn... This is so hot. I never want to wake up from this dream.

Using what few skills I have, I pick back up with slow movements of my mouth, slurping the huge cock, letting it hit the back of my throat and ignoring the reflex to gag. Hollowing my cheeks, I suck harder and the groan happens again.

And then I notice fingers, sliding up my jaw and curling at the nape of my neck.

He's holding me in place. *No,* he's trying to stuff himself deeper.

My dick pulses again, and I let him guide me, fucking my mouth with gentle thrusts as I lie there and take it, swallowing on him until I hear a hushed, "*Fuck...*"

My eyes flutter open again, and I tremor when I find him staring down at me, his own gaze hooded and wanting to fall, though it doesn't. He keeps watching me, holding my eyes with his, cheeks visibly flushed even in the dark, lips parted and trembling.

Jesus, he looks good. I wish this was real...

But there's no way it is, because he's not stopping me. He's not pushing me off him and calling me disgusting.

He's as lost to this as I am.

His head drops back, and he bites his lip, throat dipping in a swallow. Which reminds me of how much spit is flowing from my mouth. I gulp on his cock once more and he whimpers.

"Fuck yes, baby," he growls. "Suck my dick."

My balls draw up. I'm so close to coming myself, from nothing more than having his dick in my mouth while I hump the couch. It's amazing, and also not, because I'm so turned on by *everything* about him. It wouldn't be the first time I came in my pants just from imagining having him like this.

At my mercy. *Needing* it, as much as I have for fucking years.

I've sucked a few dicks before, but it's never been like this. I've never wanted someone to just *live* in my throat before.

My hips push some more, the friction on my cock, and my nuts, driving me absolutely wild. I continue to suck him, *deep*, worshipping his long dick with my lips, drawing out more of those salacious noises I've been dreaming about for so long.

The thing is, though... these ones are different. There's something about them that's registering in my head.

Less echo, more presence. Vibration in his body when he whispers, "Baby, I'm... I'm gonna come. You're gonna make me come so soon."

I let out my own hum on his dick, tonguing it with fervor, taking him as deep as I possibly can until I'm so dizzy I can barely hold myself up.

A sudden spark of pain brings my eyes up. He's yanking at my hair, hard. Chewing on his bottom lip, eyes black like coal, the wide wall of muscle that is his chest pumping through heavy breaths.

This is real.

This is *fucking real*.

My lashes flutter, my balls spin out. And I fucking *come*.

Whimpering on his stiff flesh while my dick shoots off in my pants, I find myself gripping his thighs, digging my fingertips into the muscle. As hard as he's gripping my hair.

Then he shoves his dick so deep into my throat, I have tears running from my eyes as he growls, "Fuck... *yessss.*"

An explosion of thick, salty liquid hits, pulsing onto the back of my tongue and all in my mouth. It keeps the high of my own orgasm going for what feels like hours while I drink him down, sipping his flavor like the eggnog from earlier...

On this couch. Right fucking here.

When I'm done eating his load, I pull my mouth off his many inches, head spiraling like a top.

I'm fucking *lost*. There's no way that could have really just happened, but... it did.

I can taste him on my tongue. Feel him panting, and hear it, ringing through the room.

Glancing up at him, we lock eyes for several generous seconds of awkward, puzzled and blissful silence.

I blink.

He blinks.

We both blink.

His fingers finally release my hair, swiping the line of my jaw. Then they trail over my lower lip, brushing it in bewilderment that's palpable.

The calm in this moment, however, dissipates fast. And then I witness a rage grow on his face. Guilt and shame and... disgust.

Yea... It was definitely real.

Those feelings are all too familiar to me. Except I've only ever felt them in myself. Having them mirrored back to me on his face is... not fun.

So I choose to hide.

I cower, zipping my eyes shut tight and curling up into a

ball, pretending to fall back asleep. I'm not even really pretending as much as I'm wishing for it.

Praying that this was all just another one of my twisted dreams.

Though I know damn well, in my heart, it was not.

SEVEN
James

Pacing.

Pacing and pacing and pacing, in circles and circles and circles.

I think I've walked the entire circumference of my bedroom fifty times. Maybe more.

All the while, my brain teetering between an active slideshow of what happened downstairs and a mental block forcing myself to erase it completely.

I'm still fighting for some kind of hope that it didn't really happen. It *cannot* have been real.

But even if it weren't, it's equally bad. If I dreamt about something like that… then what the fuck is really wrong with me?

After what shall henceforth be referred to as *The Incident*, Jesse curled up and fell asleep. Maybe he truly was asleep the whole time, which in no way makes it better.

I was stunned for many minutes. Unable to move or speak or even think. The orgasm fog wore off fast, and I was hit with a wave of guilt and shame unlike any other. A tsunami of *bad* and *wrong* swept me under, and I stumbled off the couch, running as fast as I could while trying to remain quiet, stealth.

I sprinted up the stairs two at a time and locked myself in my bedroom. Which is where I am now... *Pacing*.

Hours have passed by the time I finally crash onto my bed, exhausted from all the bullshit bubbling up in my head. It's five in the morning and still dark outside as I crawl beneath my covers, rubbing my eyes hard with my fingers. *What the fuck even happened down there?*

Everything was normal. We watched the movie, Jesse passed out on the couch, as he's done a million times before. Then I fell asleep too, which hasn't happened in a while, but still, it's not completely out of the ordinary that we'd both conk out on the couch.

How in the holy *fuck* does that translate into... *The Incident??*

Jesse's sleepwalking has clearly taken a turn for the devious. But it's not his fault. I can't blame him for something he did in his sleep, just like I can't blame him for his sleepwalking, even if it brings him into my bed on occasion. It's never crossed any sort of line before tonight.

So what changed? What happened to turn his seemingly innocent subconscious travels into actions of the... blowing persuasion?

Jesus, I can't think about this anymore.

My heavy eyelids droop with that word floating behind my eyes.

Can't. Can't can't can't can't can't.

Cracking my eyes open, there isn't as much light as there was yesterday coming from outside. When I peer at the window, I see gray skies, snow still falling in more of a sleet form.

Great. The roads will be shit for days.

Sliding out of bed, I walk to the door and find it locked.

And recollection comes at me like a pillowcase full of dead batteries to the face.

I haven't locked my bedroom door in a while... Because of Jesse.

Yet last night, I locked myself in here to hide *from* him.

My hands cover my face. *What in the fuck is going on?*

Slating those thoughts for later, I go to the bathroom to take a shower and do my thing.

Exiting slowly many minutes later, I can't help but glance across the hall at Jesse's bedroom. The door is open, and he clearly isn't in there. *Did he sleep on the couch all night?*

Now I feel kind of bad.

It's Christmas. We shouldn't be dealing with whatever nonsense happened last night—or didn't, if we're choosing denial, which seems like a comfortable fit. We should be spending time together as a family, like we do every year.

So I go back into my room and get dressed in my *Grinch* Christmas sweatshirt—Jesse bought it for me when he was twelve, and I wear it every year—and I go downstairs, biting the bullet. Chewing on the damn thing and swallowing it with a solid gulp.

We're going to have a good Christmas. *That's it.* Even if I have to force it, *normal* is the name of the game we must play.

As soon as I'm halfway down the stairs, I'm hit with a whiff of warm sweets. It smells like Christmas cookies, and sure enough, when I round the corner to the kitchen, I find Jesse mulling about, scooping cookies from a baking sheet and placing them onto a platter that's already full.

I can't fight the way my brows lift. The entire island is covered in treats. Apparently, he's been at it for a while.

When he hears me, he glances over his shoulder, a subtle smile twisting his lips. "Merry Christmas!"

My jaw tightens, though I'm pretending I don't know why as I lean against the doorframe and grumble, "Merry Christmas. You opening up a bakery I don't know about?"

I nod toward all the cookies and cupcakes and brownies covering the island, and the counters, enough to feed several sports teams. Some appear to be finished, already decorated with frosting and sprinkles, elaborate enough that they very well could be sold in a shop for dollars apiece, while others are fresh out of the oven and awaiting his immaculate attention.

He gapes at me with wide eyes for a moment, before peeking at all of his tasty creations. His cheeks blush pink. "Um... yea," he chuckles and rubs the back of his neck. "I guess I went a little overboard."

Guilt swims in my bloodstream as I step gingerly into the room, being sure to keep my distance all the same. "It smells great."

He blinks at me, tugging his lower lip between his teeth. I can't help how it shifts me in place.

Nope. We're not doing this.

"Hey, why don't you take a break?" I murmur at him. "You've got presents to open."

Something flashes over his face, an emotion I can't read, though I can tell it's somewhere in the realm of despondency, before he covers it up with a smile and nods.

"Okay."

Turning, I stalk into the living room, where the TV is already on. Or still on, playing *Elf* at a low volume. My fingers twitch, and I close my eyes to take a breath, inhaling and exhaling slowly, reminding myself that everything is fine.

Nothing happened. We're totally good.

We're ignoring this.

Except that I can feel Jesse enter the room behind me, like someone just opened the door and a gust of cool wind burst in, sheeting my skin in goosebumps.

Fuck my life.

Wandering over to the couch, I take a seat. But then it reminds me of things I'm not supposed to be thinking about and I jump up, moving to the loveseat by the fireplace instead. Turning my head, I squint at it.

"Did you get the fire started?" I ask, curiously.

He nods, waltzing over to the Christmas tree and dropping onto his knees on the floor. "Yea. I'm not incompetent."

A chuckle rumbles up my throat, though it gets lodged in there and I clear it. "Good job, kid. That one, right there." I nod at a large box wrapped in paper with snowflakes on it. "Do that one first."

He looks excited as he reaches for it, reminding me so much of when he was a kid, it brings fuzziness to my chest that trumps all awkward discomfort.

This is what feels right. Opening gifts on Christmas morning, although checking the clock, I find that it's already almost noon.

This is good. Regular stuff. Normal.

None of that... whatever the hell from last night that's oddly settling in my balls, in a way that has me squirming in my seat.

Jesse tears open the wrapping paper to reveal the box for a Cuisinart mixer, one of the best ones on the market. He's been not-so-subtly hinting that he wants one for six months, so it was an easy buy as his big gift.

And judging by the look on his face, I made the right call.

"Oh my God!" He cackles, examining the box closely, fingers brushing over the writing. "This is the exact model I wanted!" He tilts his head in my direction. "How did you know?"

I can't help but laugh. "I'm good like that."

"Mhm..." he mumbles, grin so wide it could be seen from space as he opens the box, checking out the device.

"There's some other stuff to go with it," I tell him.

And he launches at the rest of the gifts, unwrapping things, tossing paper and bows everywhere. I also got him some baking tools, things I researched online to help him with his process. And lastly, an apron with the drawn image of a defined torso.

I thought it was cute when I bought it, but now it's sort of coming back to bite me.

He holds it up over himself. "This isn't far off from how I already look." He smirks at it, but when his eyes come back up to mine, I flinch.

My mouth fills with saliva and I have to keep swallowing over and over.

Our gazes lock, and the room grows stuffy with uncomfortable silence. Jesse doesn't seem like he's processing anything from last night. The awkwardness is coming directly from me, which leads me to believe that maybe he wasn't fully awake for *The Incident*.

And if so, that makes me the creepiest fucking pervert in the history of scumbags.

"You wish, kid." I force the witty comeback to grate from my throat, dry and scratchy like sandpaper.

He scoffs, though the amusement doesn't reach his eyes. Suddenly the entire room is burning the fuck up.

It's a million degrees in here, and I'm sweating beneath my clothes.

I have to get out of here.

"I'm gonna go shovel the driveway." I stand, stomping toward the front door, though I don't even have my boots on yet.

"But I have a gift for y—"

"I don't need anything," I cut him off. "You've... you've given me enough."

Turning, I dash back in the direction of the hall, not missing the look of disappointment on his face.

But I can't right now. I *can't*, with any of it.

I need to get out of this house before I combust.

Stalking to my boots, I step into them fast, grabbing my coat and slipping my arms into it. And when I spin back around, I find him wandering into the kitchen to watch me with wide, sparkly eyes etched in concern.

"At least have some cocoa first..." he mumbles, sucking his lower lip.

I shake my head fast. "Nah. I gotta get this done."

I gotta get the fuck *out*.

This is literally the worst thing that's ever happened. I love the kid. I love him like he's my own, and I always have. There's no conceivable reason why I should be watching his mouth and remembering the soft plush of it swallowing up my dick.

Rubbing my eyes, I dart past him, whipping open the front door.

What line did we somehow manage to cross last night? What sort of sick, twisted door did we open?

And how the hell do I close it?

EIGHT
Jesse

James has been outside for hours.

I think he's probably shoveled the driveway six times by now. And it's still snowing, so he just keeps redoing it.

Avoiding me.

It's obvious, and I fucking hate it.

I tried really hard this morning to forget about my unfortunate... sleep-blowing. As much as I don't want to forget about it, I *have* to. The only way we'll be able to survive this is by pretending it never happened.

Sure, it'll kill me inside to do that, slowly and painfully, like a withering disease. But I'm already sick as it is... Wicked and damned, lusting after the man who raised me, like some kind of heathen.

What's the alternative, anyway? I can't lose my father figure...

He's all I have. If he ends up hating me because of this, I'll cease to exist.

I woke up on the couch at six in the morning, alone. No

hope of playing that whole thing off as a dream... Not with the ache in my jaw, and the taste of him still lingering on my tongue.

I took a quick shower and immediately launched into my default distraction; baking.

I definitely went overboard, but I couldn't help it. In order to clear my mind, I went on autopilot, baking and decorating every single sweet known to man. Cookies, brownies, and cupcakes galore. It worked for a while, but as soon as James came downstairs, it became clear our *tryst* wouldn't be swept under the rug.

Opening presents with him felt normal, but the whole time he was looking at me differently. With this simmering shell-shocked hopelessness in his eyes, and an aura of dubious vexation surrounding him so thickly in the air I could almost taste it.

The guilt that settled in my gut like a brick has been there since. I fucked *everything* up. My secret obsession somehow turned into action last night, and now I'm stuck waiting for him to either lash out and disown me, or worse.

What if we remain in this tense and mortifying purgatory forever?

I've been trying to busy myself with more cooking, starting on dinner, though it's only four in the afternoon. Still, I have to do something with my hands. I have to keep moving, and working in the kitchen is really the only option I have.

Instead of turkey, I'm making a roast chicken, stuffed with my homemade cranberry cornbread stuffing, and some sides. Mashed sweet potato casserole, beet salad, asparagus. It's a whole thing.

I'm flitting about, diligently, though my mind remains outside. Out in the freezing cold where my guardian is risking hypothermia just to avoid me. I really want to bring him something hot to drink… It's eighteen degrees outside, and he's been out there for hours.

Awkward or not, I'm worried about him.

But I just keep myself focused on my tasks. Once everything is in the oven, I feed the wood stove and toss a couple more logs on the fire in the living room.

By the time James comes back inside, it's dark out. I'm on the couch, reading, my eyes sticking to the words on the page, the ones I've read five times without having absorbed a single morsel of the story.

Using my peripheral, I see him stomp the hall, listening to the sounds of him shedding his boots and wet outerwear. My stomach is in my throat, heart rate steadily increasing as I hear him rummaging in the kitchen.

And then I *feel* him approaching, entering the living room with a few clunky footsteps. My gaze lifts as he sidles up to me, arm extended, holding out a mug. I take it, without words, peering down at the hot cocoa with a few little white marshmallows floating at the top. He has one for himself, and I try not to actively watch him as he takes a sip, wandering over to the fireplace.

With his back to me, I can see how bunched up he is, shoulders tense, rigid in his stance. Closing my eyes for a moment, I take a deep breath and hold it.

I have to fix this. I have to do something, *anything* to placate him. To let him know that last night was a fluke, and it meant nothing.

Even if it's the furthest thing from the truth.

Taking a sip of my cocoa, I place the mug on the side table by the couch. "I would've gotten that for you…"

He doesn't respond. I can't see his face, but from the way he's just standing there, warming himself in front of the fire, I can barely even tell if he heard me.

So I decide to keep going; keep trying to bring back the normal. "Dinner will be ready soon."

"Not hungry," he grunts, the second the last word leaves my lips.

"That makes no sense," I argue. "You haven't eaten all day and you were just outside working for five hours. You need to eat."

He spins slowly, his eyes dark with a weighted glare. "Who's the parent here? Me, or you?"

I can't help how that question makes me fumble. "I... I don't..."

"You don't what?" He lifts an accusatory brow, clasping the mug between his hands.

Letting out a strong sigh, I stand up. Time to take on a different approach here.

Maybe I just need to give him some assurance that last night didn't happen because I'm harboring misguided feelings for him, even if it *is* a bold-faced lie.

"Well, I'm gonna eat. And then I'm going out." I fold my arms over my chest, ignoring how hard my heart is banging beneath them.

He looks momentarily stunned but covers it up quickly with a scowl. "Going *out*? Where?"

"This guy I've been dating invited me over his place to hang out," I force myself to project, hopefully disguising the shake that wants to take over my voice. "That's why I made so much dessert. I'm bringing some over for his family."

It's only ninety percent lie. Tanner definitely texted me earlier for a booty call, which obviously has nothing to do with his family. And I wasn't considering it whatsoever until things became insufferable in this house.

The emotions on James's face are locked up tight. Resentment in his eyes is swallowing up the confusion, and all I'm getting is an angry glare made up of more flames than the fire behind him.

"You haven't mentioned any guy," he grumbles, jaw ticking visibly through his words. "I asked you last night if you were dating anyone and you said no."

"I didn't say *no*." I stand my ground, riding this stupid excuse straight to hell. "I said *not much*. We aren't exclusive or anything... It's just fun."

Okay... That look is a little scary.

His eyes are black, lined with a fury that seems to be puzzling him even more than it is me, as he grips the mug in his hands so hard it looks like it could crack down the middle.

"*Fun...*" he breathes the word like a threat, then cocks his head to the side. "Absolutely not."

I can't help how my brows zip together. "Excuse me?"

"You're not going anywhere," he states, as casually as telling someone the time. "It's Christmas. You're staying right the fuck here, where you belong. With your family."

That word, *family,* has an awful lot of bite to it for something theoretically positive.

Gawking at him like he's lost his mind, my mouth hangs open in perplexity as he lifts the mug to his lips. He takes a sip, all the while eyeing me over the rim, almost as if he's daring me to protest.

I have no idea what's going on here. I thought lying about my relationship and suggesting I leave him alone would help the situation. Give him the out he so clearly wants. But now he's telling me no...

He wants me to stay?? In this bubble of suffocating awkward tension??

Now I'm really lost.

"I just figured I'd give you some space," I grumble. "After..."

My voice dissolves when his eyes widen, pleading with me

not to mention it, while simultaneously imploring me to clear the air.

But I'm too much of a coward to go there first. I'm fucking terrified, shaking down to my bones. "You clearly don't want me here. Christmas or not..."

"What would make you think that?" He blinks, sipping once more.

Don't make me fucking say it... "Look, I just... I don't know what to say. So I'm gonna go—"

"Hang out with your boyfriend?" He hisses, eyes narrowing into slits.

I gulp. "He's not my *boyfriend*..."

"Right. It's just *fun*." He places the mug down on the table with a *thunk*. "But I said no. You're fucking staying, Jesse. End of discussion."

"*End of discussion?*" I scoff. "What am I? Four?"

"No. You're eighteen, but you're acting like an ungrateful little brat," he seethes at me, shooting icy rage in my direction.

It's crippling, but now my adrenaline is jacked up sky-high. I have no idea where this stern fatherly attitude is coming from, but it's pissing me off. He's never treated me this way, even when I *was* a kid.

"Why are you being such an asshole?" My fists ball at my sides. "I just wanted to go out for a few—"

"It's *Christmas*," he says again, like that suddenly means something, even though we've barely looked at each other today.

"So?" I huff. "What's the big fucking deal? I'm an adult, I can come and go as I please."

He takes a step forward, squinting at me as he holds firm. "As long as you're living under my roof, you'll obey my rules."

What in the name of baby Jesus in a manger??

Apparently, me sucking him off turned him into the stiflingly strict Dad I never had. Or wanted.

"Are you fucking kidding?" An outraged chuckle slips out with my words. *The audacity right now, I swear.*

"No." He steps forward once more. "I'm not *fucking kidding*. I'm deathly serious."

Fury bounds through my limbs, unexpectedly. I haven't been this heated since I was thirteen and he wouldn't let me play PlayStation until I finished my chores. This is beyond ridiculous.

"You're not my real father..." I mutter under my breath, sounding exactly like that thirteen-year-old brat.

Some sort of realization dawns on his face, and in this moment, he seems to hate it and love it at the same time. He lurches forward, stalking closer to me slowly, like a predator. My pulse is pumping so hard in my ears I can't tell if I'm struggling for air or breathing too much.

"And a *real father* would let you go out on Christmas to get laid?" His voice is eerily quiet, eyes alit in their darkness.

Chills sheet my skin as I back up. "I'm not going to... I just wanted to hang out with—"

"Say his name to me," he snarls, surging closer with threatening strides. "See what fucking happens."

I'm trembling from head to toe, my eyes wide in a frightful shock. Where is this coming from? This over-protective dominance that's turned him into some feral beast, coiled and ready to strike.

A small voice, in the back of my mind, throws out a suggestion...

Is he... jealous?

No. No way. That wouldn't make a lick of sense.

But when my shivering lips utter the response to his challenge, "Tanner..."

He erupts.

Launching forward, he grabs me by the shirt and pushes me backward. I stumble past the Christmas tree, knocking a glass ornament that shatters on the floor by our feet as my back connects with the wall behind me, and I grunt, no time to react before he's pressing himself into me.

Our bodies are flush, his face mere inches from mine as he practically foams at the mouth, the gray in his irises turning obsidian, iridescent with wrath. Both of our chests are heaving, and I can taste his breath on my lips, peppermint and chocolate, winding me up and sending a jolt directly into my balls.

He uses the grip on my shirt to haul me even closer, mouth hovering over mine. "I told you you're staying right the fuck here, Jesse. You are not going to see *Tanner*, do you understand? You're. Staying. Here."

"Y-yes," I stutter, arms lying limp at my sides as I gape up at him. My heart is leaping so hard behind my ribs, I'm sure he can feel it on the solid wall of muscle that's pressing into me right now. "Fine. I'll st-stay."

We've become one with the wall. His body is draped over mine, and as cold as I'm sure he was just moments ago, there's blazing heat moving through us both.

"I want you to *want* to stay," he growls, vibrating me with his deep voice and unkempt rage.

"I do," I murmur, unable to keep the tremors out as I speak. "I want to stay."

"Do you?" His breath brushes my lips, and I nod quickly. His eyes fall to my mouth. "Why?"

I'm shaking violently, thoughts all fuzzy in my skull. "Because... because..."

"Because *why*?" He pushes into me harder.

I'm fucking *melting*.

What the fuck is going on??

"Because I'd rather be with you," I whisper the truth. The first true thing I've said so far.

His fierce gaze is stuck on my lips as he swallows visibly. "Yea?"

I nod again and choke, "Mhm."

"Good..." he hums, releasing the grip on my shirt, though he doesn't step back. He keeps me pinned to the wall, covering my rapidly thumping heart beneath his palm. He cups my pectoral muscle gently, a hiss escaping his lips. "What is happening to me..."

I don't think that statement-like question was meant for me. It sounds like he's asking himself... A war going on inside him. A bloody battle.

Then something insane happens. His hips thrust forward, slowly. A leisurely push into mine that drags a whimper from inside my throat.

The contact... *Holy Jesus*, the feel of his crotch touching mine. I could pass out.

It isn't until he lets his linger there that I notice how stiff my cock is between us.

And it's not the only one.

"God, forgive me..." he mumbles, breathless and barely audible.

And then his mouth inches, it advances... it fucking *washes* over mine like a wave crashing onto a shore.

I gasp, because I can't help it, but he eats it up like a delicious treat, lips capturing mine in bold yet hesitant suction. My lower lip is pulled into his mouth, sucked like candy before his tongue swipes it gently.

He groans. He fucking *groans* into my mouth, hands flying up to hold my jaw, keeping me still while he kisses me fucking lifeless.

I'm dead. I've died and gone to heaven. Some sort of sick heaven where you're allowed to make out with your father.

No. He's not my father. Not even one bit, especially now.

He's the man who's grinding me into the wall, fisting my hair and swallowing me like I'm the last drop of water to clench his thirst.

James's hard body ripples into mine, strong hands holding me in place while I just flutter against him like a leaf in the wind. My body is a completely useless vessel in this moment, made purely to give him whatever he wants. I'm barely even kissing him back. I mean, I know I *am*, but he's doing most of the work, gripping me, sucking, licking, and biting my mouth numb.

A raspy noise escapes him as his hips meld with mine, the long, thick shape of him writhing into my own. I can't motherfucking *believe* I'm feeling his dick right now.

I can't believe he's kissing me right now...

Of all the things I've conjured up in my mind over the years, this one takes the cake. I never could have dreamt up something like this... This level of sheer, naughty perfection.

Finally, my brain jumpstarts my body back into human mode, and I slide my hands up his sides, clutching him and hanging on for dear life as I glide my tongue over his. He whimpers, tugging my hair until it stings, panting between my lips while we devour one another.

I'm burning the fuck up. We might as well be standing *in* the fire, heat surrounding us where we writhe, using the wall for support. My hands move up to his chest, and I feel the muscles constricting beneath his shirt, his strength and his size twirling my brain into a frenzy of lust and greedy desire.

I want more. I *need* more.

More of him sucking my bottom lip, then the top, then the bottom again, biting it with tender nips from his teeth, his tongue working to soothe the pain that tightens my balls and has me clenching with an unbearable yearning to be filled.

God, please never let this stop.

But then he rips his mouth off mine, aggressive breaths flying in and out of him as my eyes peel open. I catch him glaring behind me, and just as my face is turning, he stumbles back, putting space between us.

Oh right. The window.

We were literally sucking face right next to the front window of our house. The one that looks out onto the street.

It's highly unlikely that anyone saw us, or that anyone is even out there, since it's Christmas and snowing like crazy.

But obviously those rationalizations don't matter to a father who just made out with his son.

Adoptive son. *Let's not forget that part.*

James rakes his hands through his hair, shoulders hunching over as his fingers scrape down his face and he holds it, mumbling behind his palms, "Jesus, what have I done?"

My lips part, as if there's any possible way I could speak right now. Of course, nothing comes out.

I have no words... No comforts to give.

He may have initiated it, but this is still my fault. *I'm* the one who's manifested my crush into a reality. And while in most other situations that would be a great fucking thing, in this one, it's nothing short of a terminal disaster.

"I'm sorry," he mutters, shaking his head, refusing to make eye contact. "I'm so fucking sorry..."

And then he storms out of the room, racing up the stairs as fast as his legs will carry him.

Leaving me standing among the shattered ruins of my family and broken glass.

NINE
James

It's official.

I've lost my damn mind.

Things have taken a turn for the devastating, and I can't get my brain to comprehend how or why this is happening.

I fucking kissed him. I kissed my fucking *son*.

Stop. He's not really your son.

If the only comfort I can take in the matter is that he's not a *blood* relative, then I'll squeeze onto that with white knuckles. This is the worst thing I've ever done in my life, and I need something to justify it... To rationalize.

Because right now, I'm spinning the fuck out.

When I glance at the clock, I find that I've been up here for over an hour, though it feels like it's been seconds. Guilt is whirring around inside me like a blender, crushing and whipping up everything I've ever known about myself and my relationship with my kid, leaving me with something new. Something unexpected and dangerous... Exciting in how goddamn terrible it is.

My heart is fucked, and my mind? Forget about it. It's destroyed.

I ruined us. *How did everything get so fucked up in twenty-four hours?*

But the main thing that has me seething at myself is the stuff surrounding the kiss. I pushed him... I've never laid hands on Jesse before, and tonight I did that. In such an angry, perverse and dominating way. *I'm a sick fuck.*

Not to mention, I gave him a ton of shit for wanting to go out, and then I ran away, leaving him alone on Christmas.

He doesn't deserve this. Whether he was aware of what he was doing last night is irrelevant. I took it a step further down there. *One hell of a fucking step...*

He made us dinner, as he always does. In his own caring and selfless way, he was trying to make this day special for us, and I abandoned him.

I have to go try to fix this. And as twisted as it is, I'm reminding myself not to touch him as I hesitantly open my bedroom door and peek out into the hall.

Since when do I have to give myself a pep-talk about not kissing my fucking son??

I'm going to Hell. Or I'm already there.

Jesse is obviously still downstairs, and the thought of him eating the elaborately wonderful Christmas dinner I'm sure he prepared, alone, has me stomping down the steps, on a mission I'm horrified of failing miserably.

Downstairs, I don't see him in the living room, so I make my way into the kitchen, skittishly.

I've always been a confident guy. Not boastful or anything, but I just know who I am and I'm good with that.

But right now, I'm questioning everything. I'm... *scared.* And it's so foreign it reminds me of when I was nineteen, and my best friends died, leaving me a permanent piece of them I was meant to protect over everything else.

The boy with the silvery-blonde hair, who's sitting at the kitchen island, staring somberly into a plate of food.

"Hey," I mumble, and he peers up over his shoulder, his golden eyes wide and shining.

He looks tormented, and it's all my fault. I hate that I'm responsible for that look.

"Jess... I'm so fucking sorry." I force myself to remain firm and sincere in my words. In my much-needed apology. "That was completely... fucked. I'm not sure who that guy was, but it's not me, and I can never apologize to you enough."

"You don't need to be sorry..." he mutters, confusion and duress lining his face.

"*Yes*, I do," I jump to say. "I laid hands on you... My God, that was so wrong. *Please* don't hate me."

He shifts in his seat to face me fully. "I don't. I could never hate you..."

"You should." I rub my eyes. "That was... it was wrong of me. So fucking wrong, all of it."

His head shakes. "But it wasn't—"

"No. It *was*," I cut him off. "You made this delicious meal for us, and I just ruined everything. I'm sorry..." My fingers rake through my hair. "I don't know what came over me. Maybe I'm more fucked up over losing Leslie than I thought..."

His face is ashen, eyes wide and unblinking as he just stares at me where I'm trembling with remorse at the entrance to the room.

I take in a deep breath. "If you want to go hang out with your friend, who am I to stop you? You're an adult, after all. I shouldn't have reacted that way... I don't know why—"

"You don't?" He hums. I can see his chest moving with unsteady breaths. It trips me up.

"No... I..." My chin dips, and I swallow hard. "You should

go... see..." I was about to utter the kid's name, but it catches in my throat, and I clear it roughly. "Your friend. Go have fun. And we'll just put this whole bullshit day behind us."

I catch a look of anguish on his face, but I ignore it and stomp across the room, going for a plate. I busy myself with scooping food, all the while feeling his gaze on me, like spatters of liquid heat.

Pushing it all away, I take a seat across from him and immediately dig into the food. It's...

"Delicious," I tell him, glancing up for just a moment.

His lips part, but nothing comes out for many heavy moments, before he finally mutters, "Thanks."

"I'm just gonna eat and hit the sack," I go on, gaze set on my food. "It's been... a long day."

The silence stretches over the room like a giant tarp, covering us and holding in all the tension. It's just shy of unbearable, but I fight it as best I can, because what else can I do?

Nothing. We have to just... move on. It's the only option.

When I'm done eating, and Jesse's plate is still full, untouched, I bring mine to the sink. "Don't worry about cleaning up. I'll do it tomorrow."

Glancing at all the containers of cookies and cupcakes everywhere, I sigh, wandering away. But his voice catches me once more before I can flee.

"James..."

Pausing with my back to him, I wait for him to say whatever it is he's been simmering with this whole time. But nothing comes out.

His silence speaks volumes.

I fucked up royally. I broke us.

He's never called me *Dad* before. And I always respected

that decision. He knows I'm not his real father, despite the fact that I raised him, and paperwork would tell a different story. I'm his *guardian*, meant to do just that... Guard him from the pain of the world, not create it.

And yet right now, when he says my name, it sits differently in my chest.

I have no idea what changed between us, how or why I'm now hearing my name from his lips as some sort of plea...

But I can't keep harping on it, and as much as I want to, I can't force the normal back. I have to accept that I might have destroyed it forever.

So I leave the room and head back upstairs. To my dungeon.

I've been lying in bed for hours, tossing and turning.

Sleep evades me, as it tends to. Though this is different. I even considered smoking, which I'll only ever do when I really need to get some rest. But I decided against it.

Torturing myself with my thoughts seems like what I deserve.

The television is on, volume so low it's almost muted. I was hoping the white noise would help distract me, and maybe lull me into some form of slumber. But it's not working. My mind is racing, flashing over the memories of the last twenty-four hours. The things I did... the things I let happen.

How it felt...

Despite how wrong I know it was, on every level, I can't stop remembering the feel of his lips. Soft and unsure, but packed with so much undiscovered lust, it's been bringing a steady throb to my balls for hours.

Even pushing aside the wrongness of what happened, I'm confounded at how good it felt. It makes no sense... Because I'm straight. And I always have been. I've never looked at any man in a sexual way before. It's a part of myself I was always fully secure with before today.

Okay... There was that one time I accidentally stumbled upon a video. And it may have captivated my attention for more minutes than I'd ever admit out loud before I ultimately clicked back onto something more along the lines of my typical repertoire.

But that hardly makes me interested in guys. It was just a very brief, sort of fascinating accident. Which is a great way of describing what happened with Jesse, too.

I'm amazed at how intense it was... The head, and the kiss. Both illustrious in their own ways, rocking me down to my core. I can't stop thinking about it.

My mind is twirling and whirling like a cyclone, my body itching in some need I can't for the life of me figure out, when I hear a noise.

Footsteps, out in the hall.

My heart immediately lodges in my throat when I recognize the familiar shuffling. It sounds like Jesse sleepwalking.

Squeezing my eyes shut, I listen to him fumbling outside my bedroom door, which is unlocked and open a crack, as usual. Because despite how much I know I should be putting distance between us, I can't shut him out. I'm incapable of doing so.

So he didn't go to Tanner's house...?

Or maybe he did and came back. Maybe they hooked up, and Jesse came home, like I'm sure he's done before, which I never would have noticed before tonight.

I scoff to myself in the dark. *What kind of name is Tanner anyway? He sounds like a douche.*

What the fuck is this icky, suffocating nausea creeping up my esophagus like bile? And since when do I feel this while thinking about my adoptive son dating some asshole with a stupid name?

My bedroom door pushes open, and he staggers inside. I refuse to open my eyes, but I can hear him as he stumbles up to my bed and crashes down onto it, as he does.

He nestles up into the mattress, breathing softly by my side. My muscles are bunched up tight while I lie still, subtly cracking my eyes open. His back is to me, but I'm immediately on edge at what he's wearing... Or what he isn't.

He's in only boxer briefs. The ones he wears, like mine, fitted and hugging the slim curves of his hips. Except that where mine are usually plain black or gray, his are bright green and decorated with candy canes.

Swallowing becomes difficult as I stare at his back and shoulders, the lines of pale skin glowing in the dimmed light. He's curled up into a ball, and even though the room is barely lit, I can see goosebumps sheeting his flesh.

Without thinking, I lift the comforter I'm under and drape it over him, covering his body and shielding him from the cold. But now we're only inches apart, and I can feel his closeness; smell his scent, like sweet baked goods and the Dove for Men soap he uses.

My mouth is watering, and it's so fucking confusing I feel sick. He's my *kid*... Not some toy delivered to me as a secret, torrid little Christmas gift.

Confusing... This is so confusing.

Why am I thinking about how his soft skin would feel beneath my fingers? Why am I remembering how it stole every ounce of breath from my body when I pressed my erection into his earlier?

Why why why...

Why do I reach out and touch him... just a little. Just the slope of his plump bicep... down the line of his long arm and onto his waist.

Inching closer, I rest my head on the pillow behind his, inhaling the scent of his silky hair. He always smells like vanilla frosting.

But I've never wanted a taste before today.

This is so wrong. So so fucking wrong...

My chest brushes his back, and my nipples harden beneath my t-shirt. I have an overwhelming urge to rip it off and feel more... flesh to flesh.

I'm unleashed... I've fallen off the goddamn deep end as my fingers graze his hip, the dip right before an ass so firm and round, there's no way it belongs to a guy, let alone my...

No. I'm not even gonna think it.

But I *know* it. Regardless of whether I want to admit it, I know who he is to me. Yet my dick is filling rapidly, stiffening in my sweatpants and begging to get a little closer. A deep breath would urge it up to the crack of his ass beneath those boxers.

I shiver, disgusted with myself. But I can't stop.

I can't move away, like I know I should. My fingers slide down onto a slim yet muscular thigh, dusted in light hair. My balls draw up tight at the feel of a man... His shape so obviously not female in this moment, it should turn me *off*, not more *on*.

Fuck me, what am I doing??

I need to stop this.

But before I can, Jesse's ass shifts, his back arching as he bumps his butt into my crotch. The curve drags the length of my erection, and I whimper, biting my lip to quiet myself.

He's... moving. Writhing into me, slowly. So slowly, it's like a sensual dance.

I'm crumbling where I lie in a bed of stifling heat.

"Jess..." I breathe, my voice barely existent. Nothing but a hoarse rumble of vibration from my chest into his back. "Are you awake?"

He nestles deeper into the bed, further into my front. And he nods.

Fuck.

I don't know what to do. I can barely move.

I should be leaping out of this bed and running as far away from what's happening as possible. But my body won't react to what my brain is telling me to do.

It's acting on its own.

He urges his hips back into me again, my cock weeping in my pants as he grinds on me in leisurely strokes, quivering as he goes. My shaky fingers grip his hip, as if to stop him. But I end up cupping the side of his ass, squeezing and caressing, greedy for more of this delicious friction; this forbidden sensation that's weighting my chest and melting me to him.

I can't stop touching. I can't stop... wanting more.

More more more.

My lips ease up to the nape of his neck, and he quakes, an audibly sharp hiss of breath escaping him.

Resting my forehead on his shoulder, I mumble, "This is so wrong... You're practically my—"

"But I'm not," he finally speaks, his smooth, raspy voice gracing my ears like a sweet melody. "I'm just a man you've known since he was a boy." My breath flutters on his flesh, and he hums. "But I'm not a *boy* anymore, James. I'm a *man*. A man who wants... more."

More.

My fingertips trace the waistband of his boxers. "I've never been interested in men..."

"Why not?" His ass rubs my erection again.

I chomp down on my lower lip.

Good question.

TEN
Jesse

I'm living in a dream.

It's the only explanation.

The last thing I remember, I'd gone to bed. Depressed, confused and lonely, fearing that my lustful obsession had desecrated the only peace I've ever known.

And then I woke up in James's bed.

With his hands on me, his body warming mine in a sheet of needy tingles, his soft panting filling my brain.

When I came to, I was shocked. I'm not sure how I even ended up here. But the even weirder thing is that James didn't seem surprised at all by my presence in his bed. In fact, it seemed like something he was waiting for.

Had he wanted me to come to him the whole time?

Was him telling me to go to Tanner's a test?

That doesn't seem like something he would do, but now I can't be sure. Because he's doing a whole mess of things right now that I never expected him to do in a million years.

Like gripping my ass in his strong hands, helping me move it gradually against the long, thick shape of him.

I can feel it throbbing between the crack of my ass even through the fabric that separates us. And I'm going out of my mind.

James runs his lips gently along the nape of my neck while he holds me, thrusting into me, still with hesitation, though I think he's abandoned his rationalizations.

It's good... I want him to forget what we are, just for right now.

I've been craving this for years, and I don't want him to snap back into reality. *I can't lose this feeling.*

He pulls his hands away just long enough to tug his t-shirt over his head, then returns to me, the warmth of his flesh and all those muscles molding into my back.

Exhaling a shaky breath, my eyelids flutter. I can't believe this is happening. I feel like I'm drunk, dizzy and completely unaware of everything outside of this bed. My cock is stiff, aching between my legs as I bring a hand to it, palming myself while he palms my ass.

His fingers slink into the waistband of my boxers, pushing them down just a bit as he squeezes my hip. Reaching back, my hand covers his, and I use it to push them down further.

"Jesse..." he murmurs breathlessly, his voice nothing but a deep shudder that comes directly from his chest. "We shouldn't..."

I bite my lip, hard. Because his words definitely aren't reflecting his actions as he tugs my boxers down another inch.

I move them down even more, until my cock is out, brushing against the soft comforter.

"I know," I hum.

It's true... We shouldn't. He's right.

But what the fuck is *should* anyway when you totally *can*?

"Stop me," he pleads in a desperate whisper, his fingers shoving my boxers down my thighs. "You have to stop me right now."

My head shakes. "I can't... I want it too bad."

His entire body tremors. *"Fuck..."*

Wriggling out of my clothes the rest of the way, I'm now naked and squirming. He's still wearing pants, and I want him not to be. I want to feel more than just the shape of his dick through his clothes.

I want it inside me... *Deep*. So deep it leaves an imprint on my body that'll never go away.

His arms circle my waist as he pulls me flush against his torso, their curious touch fluttering over the muscles in my front. "You have a beautiful body."

It's insane how much that comment swells my heart, pumping it in my chest until I'm rocking with the beats.

Then his fingers drift, tentatively brushing my erection until it jerks. A gasp escapes me.

He hums. And then he makes a fist around it.

And I fall the fuck apart.

My head leans back into him, back arches to thrust my erection in and out of his palm. He groans and strokes me slowly, from my balls all the way up, then back down.

"So big," he marvels, tone lost in this hypnotic state. "Long and perfect."

"Fuck me..." I pant, cherishing the feel of his rough hand jerking me slow.

That *large* hand... The hand of a man. One who's big and strong and... older.

Jesus Christ, I could come any minute. I really need to focus before I embarrass myself.

"Have you done that before?" He breathes in my ear,

stubble grazing my jaw to keep me shivering. "Have you been... fucked?"

My mind sifts through his words and his tone. I don't want to upset him... But I can't lie either.

I nod hesitantly. *No words. Solid answer.*

His grip on my dick tightens, and I whine. "Did you go to your friend's house tonight?"

This time I have to speak. "No."

"Why not?" He mumbles, grinding into my ass harder with each pull of my cock.

"I... I don't want him." My voice shakes. "I don't want anyone else."

His movements slow. "What do you want, Jess?"

Reaching behind me, my hand slinks between us to feel his erection. He releases a jagged breath. "I want this. I want... you."

He groans, "I'm so fucked," thrusting into my hand while I thrust into his. "I'm going to Hell."

Then he pulls away, leaving me bereft, needy and terrified that he realized this is fucked up, and he's about to kick me out.

But he hasn't left the bed. He simply rolled away. And I peek over my shoulder to find him rummaging through his nightstand.

When he comes back to me, I feel him slithering out of his sweatpants. He nestles us beneath the covers with his hands all over me, his long, hard dick grazing my ass until I'm purring.

I'm lost in a haze as his hands cup my cheeks, shoving me forward a bit and spreading me open. There's a pause while I await his next move, something I can't see happening behind me, twisting me up with more yearning than I've ever felt before.

And when slick fingers swipe over my rim, I whimper out a sound, reflecting exactly that.

James hums in my ear, timidly licking my lobe while his wet fingers explore between my cheeks, swirling around over my hole before one presses inside.

"Uhh..." I gasp, shifting my ass back to him for more.

"This is tight." His lips move down my neck, kissing and nipping while his finger lurches deeper. "Jesus, it's tight. My dick would barely fit in here."

"I'm sure you could make it..." I ramble quietly, breathier than I ever have been in my whole life.

"You think?" He rumbles, pressing in another finger to join the first one, pumping them slowly, the lubrication wetting me as my muscles relax.

Burrowing my heated face into the pillow, I murmur, "Mhm."

"Jesse..." His lips tickle the nape of my neck, down to my shoulder. "You really should stop me. You're the only one who can right now."

His fingers work around inside me, as deep as they can reach until they dust over my prostate. A strangled noise escapes my lips, and I shake my head.

"Don't stop," I plead. "Whatever you do... *please* don't stop."

He mutters something under his breath, then pulls his fingers out of me. Just when it was getting good, working me up. And now I'm empty and clenching.

His left hand pets my back, and I peer over my shoulder to find him stroking lube onto his cock. I'm only momentarily startled at seeing it again.

Sure, I had it deep in my throat the other night, but it's... shockingly big. And *long*.

That thing's going to be up in my guts.

A chill of excitement fizzles in my belly.

James pushes me until my ass is angled up as he kneels only

partially over my left leg, still practically lying on top of me. And then he nudges something fat and smooth up to my asshole.

And he gives it a nice shove.

"Mmm..." My lips press together as I clutch the comforter in my fist, relaxing everything below my waist for him.

He keeps pushing, fighting against my body's resistance. "I want inside this tight little hole..."

I can't help how his words make me clench. I've dreamed about him saying dirty things like this to me for years... And now here they are. Hushed, salacious words slithering into my ear.

He shoves again. "*God*, I could probably come just like this..."

You're preaching to the choir, pal.

Finally, I manage to relax enough for the head to slip in. It's so wide and round, arousal seeps from the tip of my dick onto the bed.

"Guhh." Nonsense streams from my lips as he releases a choked sigh. Then pushes in more.

I'm fucking falling...

"Holy fuck... Jesus Christ," he moans in my ear, licking and sucking at it while he drives in deeper, tearing me open wide with his girth. "Oh my *fucking God*, my dick is... in you. It's... I can't believe I'm fucking *inside* you..."

He thrusts another inch, and my eyes roll back in my skull. "Fuck... me... you're... *huge*."

His dick goes on for miles, and it takes minutes for him to find himself all the way inside me. But when I feel his pelvis on my ass cheeks, I lose all semblance of reality.

I'm burning alive, the intensity of having this massive object so deep in my body, deeper than even seems possible, liquifying me into a puddle beneath him.

James shifts, moving his hips subtly to adjust himself to the feeling. I can tell that's what he's doing because he's breathing like his lungs are shrinking and he hasn't even gotten moving yet.

"*This... this is... life-changing.*" He rests his forehead on my shoulder blade, gripping my ass hard with his hands. Then he pulls back, just a bit, just enough for us both to groan out loud. "Fuck, baby, you feel so good."

Baby...

I bite down on the pillow while fireworks pop off in my chest. *Oh, please never stop calling me baby.*

James works up a rhythm. Almost agonizingly slow, allowing me to feel every ridge of his massive cock, sliding in and out of my ass. My body is gripping him tight, not wanting to ever let go, and reveling in the feel of him fucking me into the bed. As he picks up his pace, his hips push into mine, smacking on my ass quietly while he rides me into oblivion.

"Please tell me this feels good for you," he hums, a hand running around to my front to grip my chest. "I'm going out of my fucking mind."

"Ffuuckk... me... harder," is all I can say.

My body is wrapped in a cloud of erotic fuzz, and I'm floating up into the atmosphere.

"You want it hard, baby?" He growls, sucking on my neck and biting me until I whimper. "You like how I fuck you?"

"Yes," I mewl, grinding my hips into the bed on his fierce thrusts, the friction on my aching cock sending me soaring. "God, *yes*, you fuck so good."

"*Jess...*" He fucks and fucks, harder and deeper, rutting into me with all his might, though it stays slow. Gradually rough strokes of his big dick in the tight channel of my ass. "I never knew it could be like this... I never knew it could *feel* like this... Baby, take my fucking cock."

"Unnghhh..." I'm seeing fucking stars.

He's turned me into a giant ball of sensation, my balls drawn up so tight, they're practically convulsing.

This... This is what I've wanted for years. Since I lost my virginity, and even before. I've been wanting this man for so fucking long, and now I have him.

I *have* him... inside me. Pumping me full of cock so thoroughly, it's about to come out my mouth.

James's weight pushes me deeper and deeper into the bed while he licks and sucks and bites all over my neck, my shoulders, my back. His hand is squeezing my pectoral tight, and then he brushes my nipple with his thumb, circling the hardened peak until I'm buzzing.

Jesus fuck, I'm gonna come. I'm gonna come any fucking minute.

"Tell me it's good." He flicks my nipple again, rougher this time. "This is what you need, baby... Tell me it's what you need."

I cry to him in a quiet rasp, "It's all I need. This... *you.* Fuck yes."

Pounding into my ass over and over, James's kisses on my neck drift from hungry to sensual, carnal in the way he's teasing my flesh, expelling harsh breaths on every thrust.

I force my head up and turn over my shoulder to look at him. I just have to see his face... To know this isn't a dream.

When our eyes connect, the stars align.

Nothing has ever felt this right.

I bite my lip, and James's dark eyes fall to my mouth. I witness him swallow before he inches closer, and closer, until his lips brush mine.

We're breathing so fast, so aggressively, swallowing up one another's moans and pants while he fucks my ass with his huge cock, and I take every swollen inch with unmatched pleasure.

"Kiss me," I beg, no chill and zero fucks to give. I *need* it. I need him. *All* of him.

One quavering hum is all I get before his mouth crashes into mine. He takes my lips, claims them for himself, sucking and pulling, sliding his tongue in to meet mine while he continues to pump the air out of me.

I open up wider for him, kissing him back in slow, tantalizing laps, tasting him and purring into his mouth like the desperate, needy thing I am.

James's hand rushes up my chest to my throat where he holds on, fingers at my jaw, feeling it flex while we kiss each other stupid, lust-drunk and feverishly falling from grace.

"I'm gonna come," I whisper into his mouth, my dick already twitching out pulse after pulse of precum every time he hits my prostate with that fat, swollen head.

"You gonna come for me, baby?" His hand leaves my throat, though his lips keep sucking at mine, fingers gliding down my abs to my cock. He fists it and tugs, taunting my orgasm. I nod fast. "Come in my hand, sweet thing. Give me what I want... your cum all the fuck over the place."

God. Fucking. Damn.

I explode. The orgasm hits me like a torpedo. Unlike anything I could have ever done to myself, or anything some other dude could attempt. This is all James, detonating my balls and turning my dick into a fucking hose.

Cum sprays all over the place while he milks it from me, his hips still pumping, giant cock still sliding, owning the fuck out of my ass until I have nothing left to give.

I can't fucking breathe, but James is giving me his oxygen, panting and groaning silent sobs on my lips. "You're so sweet, Jesse. You come so good for Daddy, don't you?"

"Yes!" I cry. Because yes. Yes yes *yes, Daddy... that sounds good.* "I'm coming for you... I'm coming... fucking... *everywhere.*"

"Mmm... Good boy, baby. You want me to pour into your ass nice and deep?"

My body is humming. I have no idea what's happening or where I am. "Yes. *Please...*"

"You want me to fill you up until your warm, tight hole is overflowing with my cum?"

"God, fuck yes... fuck fuck..." *What am I even saying??*

Jesus, this man... Where did that filthy mouth come from?

James's hip buck into me steadily as he sucks my bottom lip and tugs it with his teeth for only a few more pumps until I feel his cock swell to an almost irrational thickness.

And then I feel the hot spurts of liquid filling me from the inside.

"*Baby...* I'm coming in you," he croaks, bringing his cum-drenched fingers up to our mouths.

He licks some up, then licks my lip. Then I lick some. Until we're both cleaning his fingers off, tasting my cum like sweet icing.

What... in... the... actual... fuck?

Curling up into him, my ass clenches on his erection, still firm, though I can tell he's done coming. He wedges his face into the crook of my neck, breathing me in while catching his breath, arms circling me and holding me to him tight.

And we lie like this in his bed, for many quiet moments. The only sounds to be heard are those of our breaths evening out, and icy snow hitting the windows from outside. It must be freezing out there...

But in here, it's warm. Deep in the confines of forbidden land, where you get your holiday wish with no consequences.

And you can just be who you are... Free of judgement.

I'm in love with him. That's never going to stop... Especially *now*.

ELEVEN
James

Feeling truly settled is an interesting concept.

It's something most of us strive for, and a lot of times, we'll think we have it, only to find out later it wasn't all there. We had only a portion of it all along.

I'd always considered myself content. On the surface, I was happy. Thriving business, nice house, smart kid... A relationship.

But just under my skin was a want for something *more*; a need I never allowed myself to acknowledge... Until I found it.

Until it revealed itself, like a magician's final trick. Camouflaged... it had been hidden inside me the whole time.

With my eyes closed, I can still smell him, all around me. His scent has taken over my bed, but now it's more than just his masculine vanilla sweetness making my mouth water. It's the smell of *us*, together. Sex swims around me, invading my senses. Not just any sex, either...

Gay sex. *What on earth is this, and how have I never known how mesmerizing it could be until now?*

I know Jesse's not in the bed. He spent all last night nestled up against me, all soft skin and silky hair, curves of taut muscle, and warm breaths brushing my chest.

We both fell asleep shortly after we came, making no attempt to clean up our mess or clothe ourselves. No breaking the spell by slipping back into reality.

This dreamland is much more satisfying.

I woke up a few times in the night to make sure he was still here. And I couldn't help myself... My hands traveling all over him, petting him sensually, treasuring him.

I still know it's wrong. I'm not a total psycho. I'm fully aware that we crossed a detrimental line, and there's no hopping back over it. But I can't deny that I'm *settled* now...

The inner itch is gone. And it's as wonderful as it is baffling.

Was this what I needed all along?

To sleep with my adoptive son??

Pulling my pillow over my head, I groan beneath it. The things I said to him last night... Lost in the heat of the moment. I called myself *Daddy*...

Jesus Christ, I really am sick.

I'm balancing on a tight rope, between my self-loathing over my actions, and an odd acceptance of them. Part of me just wants to give in to it.

The other part knows this won't end well.

Maybe if I knew where Jesse stood, it would help me determine my next move. Last night, he told me he doesn't want anyone else...

Was he just saying that because he was turned on and wanted to fuck? Or God forbid... because I'd made him feel like that was what *I* wanted?

As fucked up as this all is, I couldn't live with myself knowing I'd coerced him into something so twisted. If I groomed him in any type of way, I'll chop my own balls off and let myself bleed out.

Rolling out of bed, I pull my sweatpants on and head downstairs. Fuck showering for right now.

I need to see him. I need to get a read on him, and make sure he's okay.

I half expect to find him cowering in a corner somewhere, hugging his knees to his chest and rocking like the victim of an assault.

But that's not what's happening.

When I turn the corner to the kitchen, I'm hit with multiple surprising sensations. Christmas music playing on a speaker across the room. The smell of even more baked goods, which isn't out of the ordinary in this house. But still, I hadn't expected it at six in the morning.

And then there's him.

My kid, whom I'm now appraising as gorgeous and sexy, standing by the counter, mixing something in a bowl. He's wearing the apron I got him, and some fitted yellow boxer briefs with bananas on them.

That's it.

Biting my lip, I can't even comprehend the sight of how those ridiculous things hug the curve of his perfect ass. Or why I'm suddenly lusting after the ass of a *man*... A much younger one. One who also happens to be my *son*.

Wanna kill an erection quick? Remember changing the diapers of the person you're ogling when he was a baby.

Yea, that'll do it.

But even so, when he turns to face me, wearing a beaming smile and a stupid apron I bought him with the cartoon illustration of a muscular torso, honey-colored eyes shimmering and light hair all tousled about, it brings the throb back to my balls post-haste. And my chest.

I guess I'm more fixated on who he is now than what I

remember of him as a child, which is a very fucking good thing for my sanity.

"Hey," he chirps, chomping down on his lower lip to stifle his eager grin, though I can read the excitement on his face.

He's not depressed or tortured over what we did.

He's *happy*.

"Hey," I mumble, shifting my weight back and forth.

I'm so out of my element right now. All I want is to go to him, touch him some more, kiss those plush lips and hold his firm body against mine until he melts right into me.

I'm awestruck at this craving I have for him now. Where did it come from? Did it just pop up out of nowhere, or was it always there, and it only just made itself known?

Glancing at his newest creation, I note a couple familiar ingredients. "Pumpkin pie?"

"Yes, honey bunch?" He smirks, then cackles out loud at the look on my face. "Sorry, I couldn't resist. No, it's your favorite."

"Ah," I sigh, waltzing closer to observe. "Blueberry."

"Mhm." He spins back to his task. "With the brown-sugar toasted pecans."

"Yummy," I murmur, moving up behind him.

He peeks over his shoulder and lifts a brow. "Very."

I stop myself before I can attack, fingers twitching at my sides with the need to grip that luscious booty. I can't stop remembering how fucking mind-blowing it felt to pump into him last night... His tight body squeezing the life out of my cock. The sight of it alone is burned into my brain forever... Watching myself disappear inside him.

Jesus... I'll never need to watch porn again as long as I'm alive.

And I'm momentarily stunned at how stiff my dick is

becoming at the pictures in my head. Stroking his long cock, touching his balls. Pushing deep into his warm, snug little ass.

Am I straight? Because seriously, I couldn't pick boobs out of a lineup right now.

"Are you going to touch me?" His voice startles me out of my head. I blink at him as he pushes his butt out. "The waiting is driving me a little nuts."

Letting out a ragged breath, I reach forward and grab his hips, yanking him into me until his perfect ass is on my crotch. My erection is already standing tall, fighting against the material of my sweats. Jesse leans back, melding his back with my chest and resting his head on my shoulder, showing me the slope of his throat.

His Adam's apple dips, and my teeth set with the desire to suck and bite him there. His pale flesh would look so good decorated in some purple marks.

How am I suddenly a teenager again??

Dropping my mouth forward, I tease his neck with my lips until he's shivering, gripping the countertop in front of him while he grinds his butt on my erection.

"Are you okay?" I breathe my question on his sweet skin, tongue sneaking out to taste him. "I mean... with everything that happened?"

"Oh, I'm more than okay," he rumbles, reaching for one of my hands and bringing it around front... to his cock. "I'm living the dream."

I can't help but chuckle. "Jess, I'm being serious. I need to know that I didn't like... force you into anything last night."

He pauses his movements, peeking up at me. Then he spins to face me, resting his butt against the counter and folding his arms over his chest. "Did it seem like you forced me into it?"

I gape at him for a moment before shaking my head. "No... not really."

"Not at all," he argues, head cocked to the side. "James, this might come as a bit of a shock to you, but what happened last night... I've been wanting it for a while."

I'm speechless. I really had no idea...

"I guess you hid it pretty well, then." I clasp his arms in my hands to unfold them, my fingers sliding down to his. Lifting his hands, I place them on my chest, the feel of his warm palms tightening my nipples. "What am I supposed to do with you now?"

He tugs his lower lip with his teeth. "There's a lot you could do..."

"Mm..." The hum slides up my throat as I watch his mouth, before my eyes drift down to what he's wearing. "That apron really is ridiculous."

He lets out a boom of a laugh that squeezes my chest. He looks so beautiful when he's smiling, cheeks flushed, perfectly straight white teeth... He's really fucking pretty. Adorable and sexy in his sheer gorgeousness. And he has a great laugh.

All these things I'm noticing... It's like a revelation. Not only am I finding myself so magnetically attracted to a *man*, but he's also my kid. And for the first time in the last two days, the taboo of this notion isn't making me want to run and hide...

It's making me hard as fucking stone.

"Don't distract the chef while he's working." He gives me a scolding tone, though he's grinning up a storm, dazzling me as he does.

He shifts and reaches over to the pie filling in the bowl, swiping his finger into it. Then he holds it up to my lips.

"Taste," he rasps, almost pleading with his eyes and that sultry voice, like sex for my ears.

Wrapping my lips around his finger, I suck the flavor off, sweet and tart blueberry bursting on my tongue. Even after it's gone, I keep sucking, holding his gaze. His pupils dilate, lips parted as an eager breath rushes from him.

Hips surging forward to grind into his, I remove his finger from my mouth and reach behind him to take some filling on my own finger. My larger body is draped over his, pressing him into the counter while I give him my fingertip to suck, and he does, greedily. Reminding me of last night, when we both lapped up his cum from the same fingers.

I'm going out of my goddamn mind.

Jesse sucks my finger thoroughly, whimpering as he goes until I tug it back, immediately grasping his jaw and pulling his lips to mine. In this moment, I can't not kiss him. I'm not sure anything could keep me from licking in his delicious mouth, giving him my tongue and groaning when he flicks it with his, lazy in his lustful strokes.

We're swallowing each other up, moving together, breathing together, sucking and biting and tasting and just bursting into flames with our mouths working hungrily.

"You're so fucking sexy, baby," I purr to him, reaching behind him to untie the apron. "I don't know where you came from... But you're just so damn tasty. I want to eat you the fuck up."

A rugged moan quivers his lips beneath mine. "I'm here, James. Devour me."

Humming a sound of pure carnal starvation, I suck his lip once more, before letting it go with a snap, yanking the apron up over his head. I toss it onto the floor, then slip my fingers into the waistband of his boxers, tugging them down slowly, kneeling as I do.

Jesse's face is priceless. His eyes are wide, shining with anticipation as he steps out of his underwear, leaving him naked and standing above me like the beautiful treat he is. My eyes land on his erection, right in front of my face, stretching long and thick, up to his navel.

I never thought I would look at a dick in such severe appreciation, but I am right now. His is perfect.

Proportionate, pale complexion only slightly darker than that of the rest of him, a blush pink crown atop his many inches, like a piece of candy waiting to be sucked. I can't believe how blessed he is... I mean, I'm big, I know that. But I'm also a much larger man than him. He's packin' heat, and it's fully hypnotizing.

"My eyes are up here," he teases, and when I give him a little scowl, he chomps onto his bottom lip, awaiting some sort of punishment for that snarky comment.

Maybe that's what he likes... Or maybe it's what he wants from me.

His *Daddy*.

God, that's so weird and creepy, but also somehow hot as fuck.

I think I have issues.

But there'll be plenty of time to unpack my problems later. For right now, I want to try this out...

Grasping his erection, I aim it toward my lips. Then I extend my tongue, fluttering it over that swollen pink tip.

"Goddamn..." he gasps, head instantly lolling back.

I smirk. *Okay... he likes that.*

So, I do it again, this time curling my tongue around it, licking and licking until I can see him trembling before my eyes. I lap some lines up and down his solid flesh, and as he's crumbling into the counter behind him, I clutch his balls with my fingers and grip them tight.

A whine bursts from his lips as he flinches, peering down at me with wonder in his eyes. He doesn't even need to speak... I know what he's thinking.

He likes a little bit of hurt.

"Don't forget who's in control here, sweet thing," I murmur at him, squeezing his sac harder while sucking the head of his cock into my mouth.

"Holy fuck... *yes*," he cries quietly. "You are. You're in control."

I hum on his erection, sucking him deeper. I have no idea how to suck a dick. I've obviously never done it before. But I've gotten enough blowjobs to understand the premise. And while I never even imagined myself performing one, I think I get the hang of it pretty quickly.

Relaxing my jaw, I suck him hard, hollowing my cheeks while pumping him in and out of my mouth. When I allow his long dick to drift further, the tip nudges the back of my throat and I fight a gag. Jesse groans, his fingers sliding along my jaw as I keep going, ignoring the urge to gag again and again to take him deeper into my throat.

Fuck, this is hot. And the notion of me, on my knees in the kitchen, sucking his dick has me going out of my mind with how forbidden it is. It jacks up the heat in my loins until my cock is leaking, begging and pleading for some attention of its own.

But I'm focused on Jesse. I want to get him off with my mouth, the way he did to me the other night. I want to suck him so good he has no choice but to pour his entire orgasm into my mouth like a reward.

My fingers massage his nuts, tenderly, yet occasionally bordering on harsh, which he seems to love. His knees are wobbling as he struggles to keep himself upright, resting his weight on the counter while I bob in front of him. I'm in a fucking daze, lost in my movements, barely even aware of my surroundings as I fuck him with my mouth, using my lips and my tongue to really work him over. I've taken to this process surprisingly quick, gulping him back like it's *my* job, not just *a* job.

My jaw is numb, and spit is flowing from the corners of my mouth, but I don't even care. I want to taste him. I want him to...

"Come!" He gasps, fingers twisting in my hair. "I'm fucking coming... holy oh my God..."

He's rambling nonsense as his dick swells up and pulses, streams of his salty flavor hitting my tongue. I swallow it as it continues to pour, filling my mouth until I'm almost overflowing. But I fucking *love* it.

Jesus, I love this. Who knew?

When I finally pull off of him, my head is spinning. And clearly, I'm not the only one. Jesse can barely breathe, sputtering as I stand up on shaky legs, my twitching fingers sliding through all the sinews in his abs and chest.

"Babe..." he mewls, lashes fluttering up at my face. "I'm falling..."

He collapses into me, and I hold him up, making a snap decision to grab him by the waist and hoist him up onto the counter. His body shoves things out of the way, but neither of us seem concerned with that as his long legs spread to make room for me.

I wedge in between them, reaching the perfect height for my crotch to rub on his.

Oh yes... This will do just fine.

"You're so fucking beautiful," I tell him, lost to the lust and need coursing between us like an electrical current.

He gazes up at me from where he's leaning back on his elbows on the counter, face all flushed and hazy. Curling my fingers at the nape of his neck, I pull his mouth to mine, hovering over him to kiss his lips gently. He gives me his tongue, eager to taste himself in my mouth. His lips kiss mine in slow motion, sleepy in his movements.

But I'm not done with him. *Not even close.*

Dragging my mouth down his jaw and throat, I suck him there a few times, urging myself to move on before I leave a mark, drifting down his chest. I swipe his nipple and he flinches, his fingertips gripping my shoulders while I circle the pink peak with my tongue, sucking it into my mouth hard.

"Ffuck." His hips buck, cock flinching back to life.

Sucking and biting some more, I kiss the curves of his pecs before giving the other nipple some attention. "You like this, baby?"

"Yes." His head falls back. "God, yes, so much..."

"You want me to take care of you?" I croon to him in between teasing and nipping, until he's vibrating beneath me, dick filling once more before my eyes.

"It's all I've ever wanted." His fingers brush through my hair absentmindedly, swelling my chest with his loving touch and his words...

It's all so fascinating. That I could feel this with him... I'm amazed at the bliss.

Leaving his nipples tender and soaked in my saliva, I graze down his abs, biting and licking through all the lines, down to the V-shape in his pelvis. But this time, I bypass his cock and move to his balls, swirling my tongue on them before sucking one into my mouth.

This is fucking insane. Animal urges are driving me, moving my mouth between the crack of his ass while I spread him apart with my hands. My shaky hands...

God, I'm possessed by this need. It's the most intense sensation I've ever felt.

Licking a line down Jesse's taint, I peek up at him, and him down at me. He bites his lip, and I suck mine.

And then, crouched down to get the perfect angle, I feather my tongue over his asshole.

A strangled hum escapes him as I drape his legs over my shoulders, licking around and around, fluttering my tongue on his rim, in the same spot I fucked last night. Where I came in him, only a few short hours ago.

Where I'm going to come in him again, as soon as I've had my fill.

"Sweet boy," I growl into his body while he quakes above me, "Your tight hole is so very delicious."

"Fuck fuck fuck…" Jesse chants, gripping the edge of the counter with white knuckles while I eat him alive.

Lapping at him like I would eat pussy, I keep going, shoving my tongue inside until he's nice and relaxed. *My sweet feast…* He's so eager, it ignites an inferno in my blood.

Finally, standing back up, I swipe my mouth with my hand and push my sweatpants down, stepping out of them while holding his legs apart.

"Lube…" I rush the word out on a breath. "I need lube. I need to fuck you."

Jesse's chest is heaving as he blinks up at me. "C-coconut oil." He nods right.

My eyes dart to the jar and my brow quirks. "Naughty little baker, huh?"

He palms his cock, eyelids drooping in arousal. "Yours."

"Fuck, that sounds good." I grab the glass jar.

Unscrewing the top, I scoop out some of the soft oil, massaging it onto my erection. Then I swipe my fingers between his cheeks, his hole puckering at my touch. With the scent of coconut in the air, I pull him closer by his thighs, nudging my erection up to where he's waiting anxiously for it.

The first push sets us both ablaze.

"Unngghh…" His eyes roll back as my head slips in.

I give him another inch. "Fuck yea, baby. Take my cock."

Thrusting in deeper, his body squeezes me tight, holding me in almost unbearable heat. I push in more, and more, deeper and deeper, watching with greedy eyes as he swallows me up.

"You look so good taking me in," I breathe to him, sliding my hands up his waist.

He lifts his head and gazes down at where we're joined, cupping his balls while I give him the final push, getting seated between his legs. All the way up in his body and fucking *loving* it.

"I love your dick deep inside me," he purrs. I shift my hips, and he groans, cock flinching on his abs. "Right there... *yes yes yes.*"

"That's the good spot, sweet thing?" I lean over him, drawing back and thrusting in again.

A strangled sound erupts from his lips as he reaches for me, gripping my arms. "Fuck me..."

Developing a slow pace, I pump into him, watching his face and his dick while I ride him out. I take his hands in mine and place them on my chest, where he immediately squeezes my pecs, tweaking my nipples.

"Who fucks you good like this, baby?" I growl, driving into him harder.

"Y-you... you do." He's visibly coming undone as he whimpers, "*Daddy.*"

This time, *my* eyes roll back.

My cock has never been harder, stroking in him, tearing him apart and fucking struggling to breathe while I pump the air from both of our lungs.

"Daddy fucks you good, right?" I'm barely even aware of the filth pouring from my mouth.

But Jesse loves it. He's trembling all over, precum leaking

out of his cock, making a sexy mess between us as I hover over him, grasping his jaw.

"Look at me, baby."

He does, eyes fighting to stay open to hold our deep gaze, my hips smacking his ass over and over, turning him out while he mumbles incoherently, "I love how you fuck me, Daddy."

"God fucking damn, I'm gonna come..."

I force myself to hold back, but it's crazy difficult. All I want to do is pour my orgasm deep inside him. But I want to get him off again first.

"Come in me." He pulls my lips to his until I'm draped over him, fucking him on the counter as hard as I can, holding him up so I don't hurt him. "*Please* come in me, James."

"Uh-uh." I shake my head, then bite his lip until he flinches. "You first."

His lips move on mine. "I'm so close."

Kissing him rough, I wrap a fist around his erection and tug to match my strokes, diving deep in his warmth, teasing the wet underside of his crown with my thumb. His breathing is out of control, panting and gasping and groaning escaping us both as I burrow every inch of myself into his tight ass.

The sounds of us fucking ring through the room, the slapping of my pelvis on his cheeks, the animalistic growls, things from the counter scattering onto the floor. It's unlike anything I've experienced in my thirty-five years of life.

I'm coming undone, ready to burst as Jesse cries, "I'm gonna come... I'm gonna..."

Resting my forehead on his, my eyes lock between us. "Be a good boy and come for me."

His entire body tightens, coils up, winding and winding until he snaps.

And his dick shoots cum everywhere, spraying it all over

both of us while his hoarse voice stammers, "I'm coming, Daddy. Yes yes *yessss...*"

"Mmm... *Good boy.* Come hard for Daddy."

His fingers dig into my flesh, bruising me in the best possible way while he unravels in my arms. I can't even take it anymore.

My balls seize and I erupt, cum bursting from my cock, pulse after pulse, deep in his ass, his sexy body taking every drop.

"Mmmm... *baby...* You make me come so good." I kiss the words onto his lips, sucking and biting him while I spin out.

"I do?" He gasps, sensually rubbing me all over; my chest, my neck, fingers twisting in my hair.

"Yes, sweet thing," I mumble to him as the world finally evens out. "You're fucking *perfect.*"

He hums an easy sigh of contentment, like that statement pleases him more than the explosive orgasm.

I'm captivated, slayed in this moment, unsure of what to think.

Being with him is... It's like living on a rainbow.

He makes everything good.

How is it possible that this is the same kid I raised from the time he was two?

My fingers trail his jaw while we kiss for a while, catching breath and giving it to each other, coming down from our high and sweeping straight up into another.

"I want this always..." He murmurs sleepily, legs locked around my waist, clinging to me.

I move my kisses down his jaw into the crook of his neck, to smell him and treasure him, but also because I don't know if I can look at him right now. This whole thing is throwing me for a loop.

When I finally lift myself up on shaky arms, I pull out of

him slowly, buzzing head to toe at the sight of my cum dripping from his ass. He's flushed all over, pale complexion the sweetest shade of pink. Glancing at his throat, I notice that there is a small purple mark there...

I left a hickey on him.

Fuck. I wasn't supposed to do that.

I help him down from the counter, but when I go to release his hand, he holds mine tighter. There's so much longing in his golden eyes, so much he clearly wants from me, and I just don't know if it's possible to give it to him.

My eyes fling to the window next to us, above the sink. One of our neighbors is out there, shoveling his driveway.

My heart lodges into my throat.

He never would have seen anything. It's too far away. Plus, Jesse was lying on the counter, out of view of the window.

But even that trips me the fuck up.

What if the neighbors did see? What if *anyone* saw??

I've been raising this kid since he was two. I'm not supposed to fuck him. It's like the number one rule.

Despite these new feelings spreading inside me, confusing me down to my core, it's still wrong. It's *so* wrong and no one could ever understand.

"Stop," Jesse mumbles. I look up. "Please stop. I can see you shutting down... Freaking the fuck out over this. Please, James, don't do this..."

I shake my head. "Jess... It's so wrong, though. No matter how good it feels in the moment... the forbidden thing... It's fucked up. We shouldn't be doing this."

"So it's only hot to you because it's forbidden?" His forehead lines in hurt.

"No... yes... I don't fucking know." I rub my eyes. "I have no idea what's going on."

"Well, I do," he snaps. "I've been in love with you since I

was like fourteen. I know it's wrong. I *know* that... I'm not stupid. But it changes nothing." He pulls me by my hand until I stumble into him, and he wraps his arms around my waist, holding me tight. "I don't care what anyone else thinks..."

For just a moment, I mold myself to him. I hold him back and rest my chin on top of his head, letting how *right* this feels wash over me.

He's been in love with me...?
Do I love him, too?
Do I want to be with him? Could I?

But my fear, my utter terror at what anyone in the fucking world would think about this, zips up my spine, and I break out into rampant chills.

I wriggle out of his hold. "It's not just about what the world thinks, Jess. It's about what *I* think... *I* know it's not right."

"How is this not right?" He hisses, eyes wide and shimmering sadness. "Explain it to me... Because it sure as fuck feels right when we're together... doesn't it??"

I nod solemnly. "But it doesn't matter, Jesse. You said you've been in love with me since you were fourteen? Well guess what... I was your *father* then. I still am now, whether or not you're an adult. Legal fucking documentation states that I'm your fucking father. Even if we don't share blood, even if you don't see it that way... It's still the truth. I can't... I can't look past that." I let out a breath, heavy with devastation. "Even if I want to."

I despise the look on his face. It's ridden with so many emotions, none of them good. Anger, frustration, sadness, guilt, shame... It's all there, and it's all awful.

"So you're too afraid to say fuck you to society?" His voice quivers. "For me?"

"I... I don't know if I can..."

My heart is sitting weighted in my gut, like a bowling ball. I watch Jesse's eyes water as he reaches onto the floor, gathering his boxers and stepping into them fast.

"Well, then I guess it doesn't fucking matter, does it?" He storms past me, and I'm *dying*.

I need to call after him. I need to tell him I'm sorry, and that I do love him... even if it doesn't make sense.

But I can't.

I don't want to lose my son, and I don't want to lose this new love before I even get to truly experience it...

But I just know I'll end up losing both.

TWELVE
Jesse

I have to get out of here.

Just hiding out in my bedroom isn't cutting it anymore. I need to leave.

I need space and I need to figure out what the fuck I'm doing.

For some reason, the last two days have flipped a switch, and things I've been wanting, *craving* for years, have come to fruition.

But it's not glamorous. It's not happy and sexy and exciting anymore, like it was only a couple of hours ago. Now it's damaging, and painful. It *hurts*.

My heart feels like too much for my chest, and my stomach is in knots as I get dressed in jeans and a pullover. I texted Tanner, asking if he wanted to meet up... and I don't know why.

I don't want to see him. I don't want any of the mildly entertaining things we've done together, in secret, of course, because no one can ever love me out in the open, apparently.

I'm nothing but a dirty tryst, to everyone, and I can't fucking take it anymore.

But I don't know where else to go. All my other friends are busy with their families or their relationships. The only person who's been consistently texting me is Tanner. Because he wants to get his dick wet.

I understand that. I know he's using me, but at this point, I'd rather be used by some dumb jock who means almost nothing to me than the man I live with... The man I'm hopelessly in love with, who can never give me back what I'm desperate to give him.

So I rush downstairs and step into my boots, praying James won't notice as I shrug into my coat and grab my car keys. He's probably off in some corner of the house, hiding from me anyway.

Whipping open the front door, I step out into the frigid air, trekking down the snowy steps as wind pelts sleet at my face. It's afternoon, but somehow dark from the weather, the skies gray and rippling with cold, icy condensation. I stomp the walkway as fast as I can while still trying to be careful, not wanting to slip and fall. James put salt down everywhere yesterday to combat the ice forming, but it's still there.

Jumping into my car quickly, I start the engine and it roars to life. I have an STI, a little beast of a sedan in cobalt blue that James got me last year for my birthday. It's fully loaded and pretty much the most badass thing ever, though right now I can't appreciate any of that. I'm too focused on getting the fuck out of here. Escaping the bullshit piling high in my life to the point of suffocation.

My breaths are heavy as I give the car only a moment to warm up before I'm backing out of our driveway.

The second I get onto the main road, I'm nervous. The roads are really bad. My car is all-wheel drive, a necessity living in Maine, but still. I can feel the tires slipping as I pull off, picking up speed quicker than I normally would in these conditions, because I'm so fucking eager to put distance between me and that house.

The radio station is still where I last left it, playing Christmas songs at low volume. That Wham! song they play to death is on, and right now it's really irking me more than it usually does. The lyrics are crooning about giving your heart to someone special, and I want to retch.

This fucking sucks.

Glancing at the screen, I contemplate switching to one of my playlists through the Bluetooth. I want to rage right now. I want angry music about heartbreak, not this dumbass whining in my ears. But I can't take my attention away from the roads. My wipers are on mid-to-high speed, and it's still difficult to see with all the snow and sleet flying at my windshield, practically blinding me.

Driving for only about a mile, my speed picks up, and I'm so distracted by the bleak state of my life, I barely notice my foot pressing further and further down on the gas.

I can't believe how stupid I am. I can't even fathom that all of this is happening as a result of me crossing a line in my *sleep*.

This is what happens when you stifle your subconscious for so long. When you want someone so badly it blurs out everything else, and you end up stumbling over the edge of rational thought and action, into the exact thing you've been keeping locked up tight.

My heart worked with my brain and my body, conspiring to fuck me over. And that's exactly what happened.

I fucked *everything* up, and I'm sick over it.

What did I really think would happen?? James would hook up with me a few times and realize he loves me back, as more than a guardian? That he would throw caution to the wind and agree to *more* with me, just because of how badly I want it?

As angry as I am, he's right. *No one could ever understand...*

Look at Woody Allen, for fuck's sake. He married his adopted daughter and has been permanently labeled a creep. And he didn't even raise her from that young, I don't think!

I mean... I'm not sure I want to compare James to a creepy old man, or me to... whoever his child-wife was, regardless of how popular his films are. I don't even know... I'm just... Losing it.

Ugh. *Fuck this.* Fuck love, fuck feelings, fuck the best goddamn sex I've ever had or could ever imagine... *Fuck everything.*

Speeding the street with my head fogged by nonsense, I hit a patch of ice, and my car swerves. The steering wheel vibrates from the traction control, the tires attempting to grip at a surface too slick, and I fishtail.

Not much, but still. It scares the fuck out of me.

And something flashes through my brain.

Something I don't particularly remember, though I know it happened... just like this.

Two-year-old me in the backseat of my parents' car, strapped into my car seat and shivering with fear. My parents losing control of their vehicle...

Skidding off the road, directly into a telephone pole.

I'm not sure how it happened. I never needed the grisly details of my parents' deaths. All I know is that they both died that night.

They died doing the same thing I'm doing right now. And that horrific moment, that flit in the blink of an eye, changed the course of my entire life.

It brought me to where I am right now...

Sliding on ice.

Terror racks my limbs as my car collides with a snowbank.

The car comes to a jolting stop, and nothing is damaged. I'm not hurt. I don't think I was even going that fast.

But I'm fucking *shaking*. I'm struggling to breathe, tears welling in my eyes as I look around, seeing nothing but white all around me, just barely remembering to shift into park. I've never been so afraid in my life.

And I think I'm having a panic attack. *Great*.

Whipping off my seatbelt, I fight to calm myself down. My heart is racing at a dangerous pace as I curl at the waist, holding my head in my hands and just trying to pull in air, though it's not enough.

My body is convulsing with tremors, icy cold hands gripping at my throat and my face.

Breathe, Jesse. Just breathe.

You're fine. You're alive.

Sobs gasp from my shivering lips, tears flowing down my cheeks. My parents are gone... They fucking *died*, and I never got to know them. It's something I've carried for sixteen years, and I think I brought that into my relationship with James.

I've always been acutely aware of the fact that he isn't my father. He tried his best, and he did a damn good job giving me everything I could ever need as a child, into a teenager, and now into an adult. He's been nothing but supportive and loving, no matter what.

It made me fall in love with him when I shouldn't have. It made me want him for something else... As anything but a father.

But he doesn't feel the same. He never will, and that's the most devastating part. Because if I can't even have him for what he is to *me*, then what was the point of losing my real parents?

"Why..." I cry harder and harder, banging my forehead on the steering wheel.

Just... *why?*

Sudden lights in my rear windshield catch my attention. I look up with wet eyes, vision blurred, at a large SUV that's stopped right behind me. A Good Samaritan, likely stopping to make sure I'm alright.

I cry even harder.

I'm not *alright*. Not even close. I'm fucking lost.

I barely process the large form staggering up to my window as I wipe my eyes frantically, trying to look less like a fucking infant crying in my car. But rather than just knocking on it, the person yanks open my door.

It's James.

Holy fuck, now I'm shaking all over again.

"Jesse, oh my God." His voice breaks as he reaches inside the car and grasps my face with cold hands, looking me over for any sign of damage. "Are you alright?? Are you hurt?"

My breathing is still too labored to answer him. So I simply nod. And keep nodding while he launches his entire torso into the car and takes me in his arms, hugging me to an almost strangling degree.

But it feels good. It feels so good in this moment, I'm crumbling to pieces in his arms.

"Baby, I thought I'd lost you," he whispers into the crook of my neck, breath warming me as he practically climbs into the driver seat, clutching me for dear life. "I thought you were gone... I can't lose you, too, baby. I *can't* fucking lose you, too."

My cries have gone silent, but they're still there as I grip him tight, pulling him and keeping him here, because I need it. I need *him*. I need everything he is right now.

He's all I have, and he's all I need. It's tormenting, this kind of reliance. But I've never noticed how much so until I left the house today.

And he came after me...

He fucking *came after me*.

"I'm... s-so... g-glad you're... h-here..." I quake in his arms, my breaths working overtime just to get the words out.

James strokes my hair with his long fingers, clutching me to his chest. "It's okay, Jess. I have you. Just breathe, baby. You're alright."

My heart thumps to expand in my chest, breaking free from the chains of hurt, bleeding for this man. If there was ever a question as to the pain of love, a moment like this would be the answer.

It's crippling, my love for him.

We stay like this for many minutes, until my breathing finally evens out a bit, and his grip feels less like he's trying to hold me together, and more like he's just holding me. Caring for me and comforting me. Two things James has always been good at.

Prying us apart, he pulls back to look down at me, taking in the sight of my face; I'm sure nothing but wide, red-rimmed eyes, flushed cheeks and wet lips. Hopefully no snot, but who knows. I've been crying for what feels like hours.

James reaches down and pushes the seat back, shifting me effortlessly as he climbs into the driver's side of the vehicle, positioning me half on his lap and closing the door. I peek over at the passenger side, wondering if he could have just gotten in there. But it's engulfed in snow. I guess I skidded right into that snowbank, and only the left side of my car is accessible.

He gazes up at me, forehead lined with distress, dark coal eyes glistening as he slides his thumb beneath my puffy eye, then down my cheek to my lips. "You... left."

Guilt simmers in my gut as I stare at him, worrying my lip with my teeth. He tugs it free with his thumb. "I'm sorry..."

"I don't want you to apologize, Jesse," he rumbles. "Your feelings are valid. I... I didn't handle that well back there. This is all just so confusing for me. It's so... new." He pauses and blinks. "For me. Maybe you've been thinking about this for a while, but I haven't. You hit me like a Mack truck, baby, and I just didn't know how to react." He stops again and breathes out slowly. "But I handled it poorly. I shouldn't have made you feel like... loving me is wrong."

"I'm *sorry*..." I mutter again, unable to help myself, grieving in my guilt. "I know this is all my fault."

"No, it's not," he protests, but I don't let him.

"Yes, it is!" I gasp, fingers combing into my hair as I yank it hard. "Because all this time, you've been raising me like I'm your son, while I've been lusting after you like a crush. Don't you think I've wanted to stop? To just make it all go away...? Of course, I have! But I *can't*. I can't stop wanting you... Loving you. Every part. And I'm fucking sorry... I fucked everything up."

The last word of my confession barely has time to float from my lips before he's pulling me by my jaw.

His mouth crashes into mine and the grunt that bursts from my throat evaporates into a whimper as he kisses me desperately, panting into my mouth. He sucks at my lips fervently, holding me still by the nape of my neck, touching my tongue with his as his fingers slink into my hair.

"I don't want you to be sorry," he says again on bated breaths while we kiss each other dizzy. My heart is spilling out of my chest, eager to unburden itself on his. "I never want you to regret this... What we've done. What we're doing... It's the best thing I've ever felt in my whole life."

Trembling whines crash from my mouth into his while I writhe into him, the warmth of his large body and his infinitely cherishing words breathing life back into me. My mind is overcome with emotions, shivering me where I sit on top of him.

"I shouldn't have left," I tell him as he opens my coat to run his strong hands over my chest. "I just... I couldn't..."

He uses his left hand to recline the seat all the way back. "Shh... It's okay, baby. You're here. I found you, and I won't let you go again. I don't want you to... go."

"I won't," I breathe, our lips brushing. "I promise."

"Good." His fingers slip beneath my shirt to trace the curves in my chest and abs. "Because I want this, too. It's confusing and scary, but I can't stop wanting you either. Jess, you're the only thing in my life that's never really made sense... In a good way. It's like you're the most unexpected gift I could ever receive. You give me *life*, baby... You always have."

I'm fucking flying. I don't even know what to say to that, but I know what I want to do. I want to cling to this man forever.

I never want to leave him again.

Opening up his coat, I touch him the way he's touching me, feeling his strength and his size beneath my fingers, making me weak. His hands grip my jaw as he kisses me wild yet thorough, our lips dancing, surviving on one another and the heat we make together.

Shaky fingers rip at clothes, mine going first to the waist of his jeans, unbuttoning and unzipping frantically. He shifts his hips, lifting me on top of him so I can reach inside and grab his cock. It's stiff as fuck already, crammed between us. Making a fist around it, I pull it out, jerking him slow and steady while he moves to do the same to me.

This car is pretty small. Two dudes cramped in one seat is already challenging, and my neck is craned, head bumping the ceiling. But I don't even care. We're wearing each other like a second skin right now, grinding together, breaths echoing inside the car, windows fogging up at an alarming rate.

James takes my cock out and strokes it while I stroke his, bringing them together so we can rub out some yummy friction. I don't want to stop kissing him for even one second, but I can't help the way the euphoric feeling of him jerking us both together has me leaning back. Lifting onto my knees a bit more, I straddle him as best I can, still fully clothed with only our aching cocks out. He pushes me back forcefully, my ass bumping the horn.

Breathless chuckles leave us both before James leans down and licks the head of my dick.

"*Fuck...*" I purr as he sucks me in, teasing me with his tongue until I'm seeing stars.

At this angle, he can only really suck an inch, but that's all I need. It's fucking wonderful.

"Baby, I can taste you," he groans, licking and licking like he can't get enough. "I love your flavor."

My fingers weave through his dark hair, eyes closed, head back, thrusting forward to give him as much of my desperate erection as possible. And he keeps flicking at it, tongue curling around and around before he sucks me so hard I go cross-eyed.

"That feels so good..." Words tumble from my lips, eyes cracking open to watch him, visibly shaking while he envelopes me in his warm, wet mouth, beating his own dick rough in his lap.

The vibrations of him groaning on my cock are almost too much to bear. I was wound up before, and I'm winding up even more now, muscles tightening all over my body as an orgasm sizzles in my balls.

No lights, we're bathed in shadows, fooling around in my car like hungry animals with no fucks to give about anything happening outside. I can hear the sleet hitting the windows, but I can't see anything. We've created enough heat inside this car to last a lifetime.

James's fingers grip my balls, and he squeezes, the pain hitting me like a wave of something so bad it feels divine. And I stiffen, shifting my hips to his mouth, giving him my cock to suck like the sexiest goddamn human being ever invented until I break the fuck down.

The climax rumbles through me as I spill into his mouth, pulsing and pulsing in aching throbs that he catches and swallows, drinking me like sheer perfection. He's humming the whole time, like he loves it just as much as I do.

Like he wants nothing more than to taste me and savor me like a sweet snack.

My fucking brain is blown to smithereens.

For moments after I'm done coming, James laps at the head of my dick, teasing me and cleaning me, breathing like there isn't enough air in the world, let alone this car.

Without even thinking, I crash off of him into the passenger seat, then scramble over the center console, fisting his cock and bringing it to my mouth.

"Mmmm... that's my good boy," he growls, fingers brushing through my hair while I pump his cock with my lips. "Your sweet mouth is so warm and wet, baby. *God...* you're gonna suck the cum right out of me."

I moan on his dick, throating him as best I can, slobbering on him while I fuck him with my mouth, gripping his thighs for leverage. James stiffens, his grunting and panting overwhelming the music still coming from the stereo as his hips lift to my mouth. His dick slides back into my throat and he swells.

"Fuck, baby, yes... I'm fucking... *coming* for you..."

The warm salty liquid shoots on my tongue and I slurp it up like my favorite drink. He keeps my head down on his cock the whole time, pouring down my throat while I whimper and cry, muffled, dazed and high as a fucking kite.

When he's done, his fingers lazily brushing through my hair, I suck up his length and sigh, unable to resist. I drop a kiss on his crown before lifting myself up on shaky arms, resting my head on his shoulder.

He chuckles, "Did you just kiss my dick?"

Dammit. That's embarrassing.

But I don't really have any suave response to give in this moment. So I shrug. "Yea. I love him. So what?"

He tilts my face up to his with fingers on my chin. "What about me?"

"You're okay, too." I blink at him, my words teasing, though the enamored look I'm giving him prohibits me from smiling.

James leans in and kisses my lips softly, gentle in his pure captivation. He's the holder of my heart right now. In this moment, he has me, more than ever before.

I just hope it isn't too much for him.

His eyes lift and he looks around, assessing the fact that we're in a car, out in the open. Anyone could stumble upon us in this compromising position.

But this time, rather than clamming up or running away, he just sighs. "We have to get out of here."

I nod. "Let's go home."

His dark gaze settles on mine. "I mean like... out of *here*. This place... this town." I can't help the look of confusion on my face. His thumb slides over my lower lip, such an intimate gesture, I'm melting like Frosty in that greenhouse. "I wish we could just leave. Get away for a while..."

My stomach clenches in all sorts of emotions. "You would do that for me?"

His eyes sparkle as he murmurs with full sincerity, "I would do *anything* for you." Swallowing thickly, I lean into his touch. "But for us too, Jess. I would do anything for *us*."

My chest unlocks with a strong breath, pulling in his words and letting them flutter about inside me.

If he really wants us...

"Take me home," I whisper, fingers trailing up to his angled jaw. "I have something for you."

THIRTEEN
James

When we walk back through the front door, together, I've never been happier to be home.

I managed to get Jesse's car unstuck from the snowbank and drove it back, following him as he drove my SUV. The kid was scared, and I don't blame him one bit. He drove five miles per hour the whole way, and I just sat in his car right behind him, inhaling deep breaths of his scent as it surrounded me.

I won't lie and say I'm at ease in what's happening. I'm still nervous, about all of this. But one thing became abundantly clear when I realized that he'd left without a word.

I can't live without him.

Maybe it was never romantic before this crazy holiday changed everything. Actually, I'm certain it wasn't, at least not for me. And I'm happy about that. It makes me feel like less of a creep, and more like a man who's been swept up in an unexpected love.

So falling in love with your adopted son isn't normal... But what has *normal* ever done for me anyway?

It kept me alive with blinders on, with an unknown treasure hidden inside me, waiting to be discovered.

I'm not sure what this means for my sexuality, but if the

only man I'm attracted to is Jesse, then I'm totally fine with that. He's gorgeous and smart and talented. Certainly more grounded than I was at eighteen.

And where we'll go from here is still vastly up in the air. But I have to give in to this. Because if the alternative is losing him, then I'll do everything in my power to fight it.

I'll carry the weight of the world to keep him happy. That I *can* do.

We strip out of our wet boots and coats at the door, and I take Jesse by the hand, bringing him to the living room. He stands in front of the fireplace warming his hands while I throw a couple of logs on. I can't read his face, but he seems lost in his own thoughts, and it reminds me of the scare he just faced.

Jesse lost his parents to an accident, and it shaped him. The tragedy of it made him who he is, for better or worse. Though I'd say *better*, because he's fucking strong. I gave him the best childhood I possibly could, and I know I did well for the kid. But he doesn't need me...

Regardless of what he thinks, his love for me, he doesn't need anyone. I respect that immensely. I'd like to think I'm the same, but I'm not sure if it's true.

Because I definitely *need* him.

Jesse's face tilts up to mine and I can't stop myself. I grab him and haul him into my arms, hugging him tight, hand sliding up to cup his head, the other resting on his lower back. He melts into me and we just sway for many minutes by the fire.

He's not shivering anymore. I think he's warm and content. I hope he is...

After a while, he pulls back and gazes up at me, lashes fluttering as he says, "Sit. Please."

I'm confounded by his soft command, and I nod, releasing him and plopping down onto the loveseat. Jesse wanders over to the Christmas tree and bends to rustle something from underneath. He comes back to me with a small gift box, wrapped in sparkly paper with a red bow on top.

"In all the excitement, I never got to give you your gift," he says, handing it to me.

I take it with a cock of my brow. "*Excitement*... That's an understatement if I've ever heard one."

Jesse rolls his eyes, a smirk covering his plush lips. "Just shut up and open it."

A chuckle bubbles from my throat as I examine the box in my hands. I'm vibrating in anticipation...

What kind of gift could he have picked out for me?

Glancing up at him, I pat the seat next to me. His grin widens and he slinks onto the loveseat, nestling up to my side. I can't resist pressing a kiss in his silky hair before slowly unwrapping my Christmas present.

Removing the top from the gift box, I blink. Airline tickets...

I peer at him, and he bites his lip. Taking them out, I read the destination.

"St. Barth..." I murmur, my fingers trailing the tickets.

Jesse leans in, pointing to the travel date. "For New Year's." I peer down at him, and he mumbles, "Surprise," chewing nervously on his lower lip. "Is that okay? It's only a week, and I know you have time off... I just figured you could use a vacation. I mean, we both could, I guess..."

I cut off his rambles with my lips, kissing him softly, though I've surprised him enough that he gasps into my mouth. I have no idea why his timidity turns me on, why the idea that he was nervous about this gift has my heart thudding aggressively in my chest. But it does and I have to force myself to stop mauling him.

"Baby... this is so thoughtful," I whisper, fingertips trailing his sharp jaw. "Thank you so much. This is the best gift ever. Well, *second* best…"

His brows zip together, honey-colored irises sparkling at me.

You, baby… You're the best gift I've ever received.

I wish I could unwrap *him*.

Jesse's cheeks flush as understanding dawns, and he breaks our intense stare, glancing down shyly before resting his head on my shoulder.

"I made a reservation at a cool resort, but now I'm thinking maybe we should get a villa," he chirps, peeking up at me once more. "For some privacy."

I can't stop smiling. It's a bit disturbing, honestly. I don't think I've smiled this much in my entire life.

"That sounds amazing." I place the box down and reach for his waist, pulling him on top of me. His eyes widen as he straddles my waist, gripping my shoulders. "One week might not be enough. Maybe we should extend it."

He chuckles, pressing his forehead to mine. "It was just supposed to be a vacation… I didn't know this would happen. I swear to God, James, I never planned on like… *seducing* you. I was all set to keep this stuff hidden forever. These feelings…" His hands fall to my chest.

"Things happened the way they were supposed to," I tell him, cupping his face. "I think… maybe it was inevitable. This."

He pulls back just enough for us to lock eyes. "You think so?"

I shrug. "There's no way to know for sure, but I'm happy. I'm sort of terrified, but it's exciting. And this trip… I think it's perfect. The only way we'll ever be able to explore this is by getting away from our normal lives."

Jesse nods, but there's still some uncertainty shining in his eyes. "Won't it feel like we're… running away?"

"No." I shake my head, giving him my confidence. I can make it my job to placate both of our hesitations. I have no problem doing that. "We're giving in to what we want. I think you unwittingly gave us both the best gift, for *us*." My fingers press to his pink lips. "And I wouldn't mind seeing you in some sexy little swimsuit."

He laughs, shivering my insides as he does. "Mmm... pervy. I like it."

He smirks and I kiss it off his mouth, humming and sucking, savoring this... It's all so new and strange. But it feels good.

What's wrong with giving into temptation when it sets your soul on fire?

Christmas was three days ago.

And things are infinitely different than they were before the most unexpected holiday revelation ever.

Jesse and I have become inseparable. Literally. We can't seem to separate our bodies. We spend almost all day every day wrapped up in each other.

He cooks and bakes, as usual. And we eat in the kitchen together, like we used to. But they're no longer family meals... They're like dates.

We're fucking *dating*. It's bizarre. But amazing. I've never experienced this kind of bliss.

Of course we haven't left the house. There hasn't been much of a reason to, especially after being snowed in for days.

We've kept the shades down, blocking out the world while we lie by the fire or on the couch, touching and kissing and fucking...

Jesus, the fucking... I never knew I could come so much in one consolidated amount of time. The kid is insatiable, and I'm just trying to keep up. But my sex drive seems to have jump-started back into teenager mode. I guess that's what he does to me.

I suppose this is when our loner qualities come in handy. There isn't anyone knocking down our doors, looking to check in and uncover our secret relationship. We're holed up in a world of unwavering lust, and new love. It's fantastic.

Yet we both know it can't last like this... It isn't realistic. And it certainly isn't fair for me to expect Jesse to remain a dirty little secret of mine. The more we go on, the more I want to take him out. To say fuck it to society's rules and kiss him in a crowded room...

It's a need that's been bubbling inside me, more and more with every minute we spend building this relationship... Building *us*.

Our vacation couldn't come at a better time. I'm counting down the minutes until we leave for St. Barth. *I can't wait to get him on a beach.*

We're in my bedroom. We just finished packing, because even though we don't leave for another two days, we're so excited we can't even contain ourselves. Jesse canceled our reservation at the resort when he found a private villa at this super nice, secluded spot. They had an opening, which was lucky, and he pounced on it. I have to say, I'm thrilled at how he's taken over planning our little excursion. I'm such a control freak in most things, it feels nice to be taken care of; spoiled, in a sense.

And by a gorgeous young hottie, no less.

Who am I?? What is this new euphoric life I lead?

Lying in my bed, watching random TV, Jesse saunters into the room freshly showered, in nothing but a towel. My dick is stirring instantly as he finishes drying off and drops it, giving me a coy look before crawling into the bed, snuggling under the covers. He presses his smooth naked flesh to mine and I'm fucking drooling... At the feel of him, the scent of him. *Everything.*

If you had asked me a week ago if the feel of taunt muscles and a hard cock grazing my thigh would turn me into a ravenous fiend, I'd laugh in your face and call you a deranged lunatic.

But now... Well, let's just say I'm having very little reservations about revoking my own straight card.

Pulling Jesse into my arms, I position him so he's half-straddling me, our erections filling rapidly as we rub them together. He's been sleeping in my bed every night, and I love it way too much. Without even needing to talk about it, he started moving things in here. And now his clothes and shoes are everywhere. He's a permanent fixture in my bedroom.

And I suppose if he's going to sleepwalk in here anyway, might as well cut out the middle-man.

The sounds of our ragged breaths and rampant lip-sucking are interrupted when his phone pings where it's charging on my nightstand. I witness him peek at it, and my stomach tightens faster than I know how to react.

"I want you to delete his number." My fingers slide down his throat. "Fucking block him. I'm dead serious."

Jesse's grin goes sunshine bright. "But then I wouldn't get to enjoy how sexy you are when you're being all jealous and possessive." He thrusts his hips into mine until I grunt. "It's beyond hot."

Letting out a growl, I flip him fast, pinning him to the

mattress beneath me. He gasps, eyes hooded with desire, lips all puffy and trembling. *He's so fucking beautiful, I can't take it.*

And he's certainly right about my jealousy. That dumbass he goes to school with has been texting him for days, asking him to hang out, striking a fury in my veins I didn't know I could possess.

I've never been a jealous person... ever. I guess I just never cared about someone enough to let it affect me. But just knowing that Jesse lost his virginity to some asshole who keeps him a secret... who uses him as a fucktoy whenever he's in the mood... It has me bordering on murderous.

I might be projecting a little. But I refuse to believe that what Jesse and I have is the same. I don't want to keep him hidden anymore. I want the world to know he's mine, no matter what kind of repercussions I know for certain we would face.

It's a tough spot to be in, for sure. No one would understand that what we're doing isn't wrong because we love each other... Consensually. He's an adult, and nothing happened prior to that. For as much as it tripped me up at first, Jesse is insistent that I never did anything to *groom* him.

And I know he's right. I wasn't even aware of his feelings for me until Christmas.

This is the part of falling in love they don't mention in the books, or movies. You want to believe love conquers all, but if I stepped outside right now and kissed the man I raised as my son for so many years, in public, there would be no swelling music, no cheers and praise for love at all costs.

People would freak out. And I would sooner die than let anyone say anything to Jesse that could hurt him, or make him feel like he's anything but perfect.

So that's why this vacation is necessary. To take us away from the reality we've known for so long and build a new one.

Even if it's only temporary...

Or maybe it won't be.

Reaching over to the nightstand, I grab his phone. Taking his hand in mine, I use his thumb to unlock it with the fingerprint, and he's dying laughing the whole time. I'm smiling too, but I'm also wading past my waist in this obviously irrational jealousy.

Pulling up the new text from Tanner, I scoff out loud. "Really?? An eggplant, a question mark, and a pouty-face emoji?"

Jesse cackles, to which I scowl at him. His fingers trace my chest while he sighs through an unrelenting grin. "It's not my fault I'm irresistible."

"That you definitely are," I mumble, fighting my own smile as I hand him the phone. "Are you afraid to tell him you're unavailable?"

His eyes glimmer up at me. "Is that what I am? *Unavailable?*"

"You, sweet thing, are available only to me." I press a soft kiss on his velvety lips. "And I'm available only to you."

"Well, if that's not a declaration of love, then I don't know what is," he chuckles on my mouth.

Sighing once more, he types out a reply to the asshole, with me peeking anxiously at the screen the whole time.

I read the text out loud as he hits send. "Sorry, homie. We're done. I'm seeing someone. And it's serious." My brow arches at his face and he smirks. To which I laugh and kiss the corner of his mouth. "You're fucking adorable."

"Facts," he breathes, tossing the phone away and taking my jaw in his hands.

"You know *Tanner* is a stupid name, right?" I murmur in between kisses.

His sweet laugh rumbles into me. "I don't know... I kinda

liked it. Jesse and Tanner... like *Full House,* if Uncle Jesse took Becky's last name."

I squint at him. "Okay, so by that logic our names are way better... I mean, come on. *Jesse James??* That's epic."

"Epic," he continues to giggle roughly while his fingers roam my skin. "You're right. Famous outlaw definitely trumps John Stamos." I let a laugh slip, and he smirks. "Although... he *is* sorta hot..."

Grabbing his hands forcefully, I pin them above his head. "All this sass is going to get you in trouble, kid."

He writhes beneath me, rubbing my erection with his own. "Bring it on... *Daddy.*"

And only minutes later, I'm inside him, pushing and pulling between his legs, lost in the heat and the sensation of him, of us. Of everything we are together.

"I love you, Jesse," I release the truth, hoarse and falling apart so splendidly for him.

And he unfurls for me, in my arms. "I love you so hard, James."

He's mine, and I'm his.

And there's nothing *wrong* with that.

FOURTEEN
Jesse

Ten Days Later…

"My ass hurts."

James gives me a look I can read, even beneath his sunglasses. "You want me to rub it?"

I laugh out loud. "Like you need an excuse."

"Point well made, kid."

We're lying on a chaise lounge on our own private beach in St. Barth. We've only been here for a few days, but it's already been the best time of my life. Nothing but sex and good food and fun in the sun, all day, every day.

I could get used to this.

I know what you're thinking, and no, my ass doesn't hurt from being railed six times a day, though that was certainly an adjustment, what with the size and general ferocity of the man who owns me, body, heart, and mind.

We went jet-skiing yesterday, and I was showing off, jumping some of the bigger waves. At the time, it was a blast, but now my butt is sore as fuck.

Might have to take him up on a nice massage later, after we adjourn from sunbathing.

I attempt to subtly sneak out from under the umbrella that covers us, but James grabs me by the waist and tugs me back.

"Stop being fresh," he scolds, a comfortable grin resting on his lips.

"I want to get just a little sun," I whine. "I won't burn, I promise."

"Nice try," he grunts, and I pout.

He doesn't want me to get too much color, insisting that my pale complexion is sexy as all hell. And normally I agree with him. But I have to come back with at least a *little* bit of a tan. *I mean... come on.*

"Why don't you rub some more sunscreen on me, then?" I roll onto my stomach, pushing my sunglasses down the bridge of my nose. "That's always fun."

He laughs. "Oh, yea. It was even more fun for the onlookers yesterday at the jet-ski place."

I snicker at the memory.

St. Barth is an awesome place. Not only is the weather perfect, the food amazing, and the sights purely gorgeous, but it's also openly accepting of all lifestyles. There are a bunch of gay couples staying in the villas near us, which certainly helped loosen us up when we first got here.

We've been able to just be *us* the entire time, without worry. It's all I could ask for.

Here, we aren't a father and his adoptive son. We're just Jesse and James. New lovers vacationing, relaxing, and enjoying each other in ways that, let's be real, we probably couldn't at home. Definitely not in the town where we both grew up.

I'm loving every minute of it, while simultaneously dreading going back. I hate that there's a timer on this.

Pushing away the icky thoughts, I get James up and drag him into the water. We walk in, hands clasped, wading into the crystal-clear blue until we're up to our chests. And then his hands travel, and mine do too, feeling each other up like we still haven't gotten our fill. I'm not sure we ever will.

James hoists me up in the water, molding me to his strong frame as I wrap my legs around his waist. I touch the tattoos on his shoulders and arms while he kisses my neck, giving me chills even beneath the heat of the sun.

"You're perfect, sweet thing," he croons in my ear, licking up the saltwater on my flesh. "Everything about you... You're beautiful and sexy and perfect and *mine*."

"I am so yours," I tell him, combing my fingers through his dark wet hair. "Always."

"No matter what?" he hums, palming my cock over the material of my fitted swim trunks.

"No matter what."

His other hand grips my ass tighter. "I'm yours too, baby."

"Always?" My heart thumps into his through our flushed chests.

"Always." He kisses the word on my lips.

Our mouths come together for leisurely kisses, sucking and biting, tongues flicking, in our own little slice of heaven we've found.

"I never want to leave." My confession breaks when we come up for air.

James draws a line up my throat with his index finger. "Maybe we don't have to..." I can't help the bemused fluttering of my eyelashes as I gape at him. He chuckles. "What if we could stay? Would you want to...?"

My heart is racing already at the idea. James had made a comment last night, while we were lying in bed after a particularly intense set of orgasms, about extending our trip. But I just thought he meant like, another week.

"Stay, as in... stay longer?"

He shakes his head. "What if we moved here?"

Now I'm really cruising the confusion highway. "How is that even possible?"

He does a little shrug, like it's the most casual conversation ever. "I've lived in Maine my whole life... I'm kind of over it. It's fucking awesome here, don't you think?"

"Well, yea," I huff, shaking my head. "But what about your business... The house? Everything else?"

"What else?" he mumbles, dark gray irises conveying so much love and dedication, it physically takes my breath away. "You're my *everything*, baby. That's it. Just you. The house is just a house... I can sell it and buy something here. Or anywhere you want, for that matter. And my business... Well, some of the local grows have been trying to buy me out for years. I could sell and set up something here. Or again, anywhere you want."

He pauses to let his words sink in, and suddenly I don't think I'm floating in his arms in the water anymore. I'm floating away altogether, light as air, weightless with possibilities.

"None of this matters if you don't want to." He keeps talking, his deep voice vibrating into me. "But if you do, we could easily pick up and move somewhere like here. Start a new life. Be happy. You make me so fucking happy, baby, and I just want to return the favor. I want to give you the life you deserve. Out in the open."

Everything he's saying rushes over me, like droplets of running water. We can't be us out in the open back home. It's just not possible, not without a witch-hunt of judging assholes who don't understand our love.

But if we were to pack up and move here... *Well, shit. That would be a fucking dream come true.*

I can see myself living here. With him...

I could open a bakery or a shop, and he could still grow, depending on the laws around here. We could do *anything*... There's so much of life for us to explore together. And I want that with James. With the man I've dreamt of having since I was a kid.

I finally have him. I'd be a moron to let that go.

So I nod, slowly, still buzzing on all these new ideas.

James's smile goes broad as he beams at me, taking my face in his hands. "Yea? You want to?"

I nod some more. Because *fuck yea.* "Yes. Totally. Let's run away together."

He lets out a soft sigh and kisses me fast, swallowing my breaths and giving me his. Giving me his love, the love I've craved for years. It's here in my arms now, a reality we'll make together.

"You truly are the best gift I could never have expected," he whispers with his hands sliding all over.

"You gonna unwrap me?" I smirk, and he growls.

My man, no matter what.

No matter how. No matter why.

He's mine.

FIFTEEN
James

One Year Later…

"What in the holy Hell am I looking at right now??"

I'm standing in the kitchen of our house, arms folded over my chest, eyes stuck on a giant pile of gingerbread cookies on the counter.

But these aren't regular gingerbread men…

Well… I guess a *part* of one…

"If you don't know what that is, I worry about you," Jesse says, peeking at me over his shoulder while he pulls out another tray from the oven. "You might be growing senile. 'Cause you had one in your mouth this morning." He giggles at my scowl. "And I'm not talking about the cookie…"

I honestly want to smile, and laugh… But my stubbornness won't allow me to. Instead, I purse my lips to keep it at bay, shooting him with my favorite scolding look I know he thrives on.

"You made gingerbread dicks," I huff, unable to stuff down

the grin for one more second. It hijacks my mouth as I pick up one of the oddly shaped cookies, examining it.

It's honestly very impressive... *The cookie and the dick.*

"Yay, you got it," Jesse teases.

"You better watch that mouth, sweet thing." I peer at him, and he bites his lip. "Or I'll be stuffing your throat with a much bigger *cookie*."

He cackles out loud, and I'm beaming. I love making him laugh. He looks *so good*, smiling and laughing; sounds like a dream come true.

Mine.

I lift the cookie to my mouth, but he reaches over and slaps it out of my hand. "Don't eat that! It's not ready. I haven't even frosted them yet."

I pout at him while he chuckles, stepping in closer and running his hands up my chest.

"But I'm hungry," I growl, letting my hands roam his lower back, gliding down to his ass and giving it a nice squeeze. "For something *sweet*."

"What else is new?" He grins, brushing his lips over mine.

He drops a lush kiss on my mouth, and I can't help the soft groan that rumbles in the back of my throat. He's just so alluring. Just being near him turns me ravenous...

And it has every day for the last year. Since the Christmas that changed our entire lives.

Jesse and I have been living in St. Barth for the last nine months or so. After our vacation last New Year's, when we decided we wanted to move permanently away from Maine, and out of the States in general, we've been living this endless dream in a tropical paradise.

We had to leave when our trip ended, but only for long enough for me to sell my business, and our house. All in all, it took about ten weeks. We packed up our lives, said goodbye to the few people we care about back home, and moved to St. Barth for good. We found our little house, a cozy haven right on the ocean, and started our lives together...

As a former father and his adoptive son, turned lovers.

Of course, no one knows any of that. As far as the people of our quaint beach town are concerned, Jesse and I are just partners.

James McCallister and his nineteen-year-old boyfriend, Jesse Sorensen. *Yes, Jesse has always shared a last name with his real parents.*

I was adamant about that when I adopted him. I didn't want to give him my last name, because I wanted to keep the memory of his parents alive, in him.

But maybe he'll become a McCallister in the future... *If he says yes.*

These thoughts send a thrilling tickle through my stomach, and it causes me to haul him into me even closer, until our bodies are pressed together so tightly, I can barely tell where I end and he begins.

Swallowing up his little gasps, I suck on his pillowed lips, tugging them with my teeth in between feathering his tongue with mine. *God, I fucking love this kid.* So much more than I ever thought was possible. As not only my family, the most important person in my world, and the man I would lay down my life for...

But also as my lover; my partner. My treasure, my escape, my sanctuary. The man who makes my heart race, and settles me at the same time.

He's literally *everything* to me. My sweetest gift.

"Mmff..." he mumbles into my mouth from the ferocity of my sensual kisses, and I chuckle. "You're... distracting me."

"What else is new?" I grin on his lips.

We pull apart, and he lifts his fingers to brush the hair away from where it wants to flop over my forehead. Clearing my throat, I stow the urges to lift him up onto the counter and tear off that dumb apron he still always wears—the one I gave him for Christmas last year—along with his fitted Rick and Morty boxer briefs, and make him come, and come and *come*...

To show him who he belongs to. And how I take care of what's mine.

"You know... Christmas Eve is tomorrow..." I murmur, slipping my fingers into the waistband of his boxers.

"Oh... *really??*" He gasps sarcastically, and I pinch his butt. He squeals into a laugh.

"I'm just saying... That's, like, our anniversary." I smirk, trailing a fingertip toward the crack of his ass. He purrs. "We should celebrate."

"Oh, trust me," he hums, tracing the lines of my bare chest, "I have a *very* special gift for you this Christmas, *Daddy*."

A growl rumbles from me into him, my dick firming up nice, as I press it into his. "I love the sound of that, sweet boy."

The excitement on his face lights him up, and he inches in, kissing my neck and throat, I think so that he can distract his mouth from accidentally blurting out the surprise he's holding.

Jesse loves Christmas. It's definitely his favorite holiday. I mean, he loves all holidays. He'll find any excuse to decorate and cook elaborate meals, baking up even more complex desserts. Every holiday is celebrated in our house, but Christmas is a special one. Even more so now, because it is our anniversary.

The anniversary of when we crossed a line separating the two very different sides of our family. Father and son, to *partners*... Sexual, and otherwise.

It's a line I never could have anticipated crossing with him before. But now, I can't even imagine not having tumbled over it.

Who knew him accidentally sucking my dick in his sleep would be the best thing that ever happened to either of us?

"Why are you making so many of these gingerbread dongs, baby?" I ask, while palming his taut, plump ass.

"I was going to bring some to Blake and Kenneth," he tells me, still running his lips over the mound of my throat while it dips with my gulp. "You know, that couple we met the other day at the beach?"

My muscles are instantly tight. *Yes*, I remember the couple we met. I also happen to remember the way they were checking him out, subtly flirting with my partner, who's too sweet to even notice such things.

Jesse was just chatting with them, the way he does. Sort of innocently, answering their questions and being polite, while I was standing there, glaring behind my sunglasses. To be fair, it's not like they were actually hitting on Jesse in front of me... In fact, it seemed like they were sort of trying to flirt with *both* of us. Maybe part of their holiday vacation in St. Barth is finding another couple to fool around with... And Jesse and I became their prime target.

Jesse didn't pick up on it, apparently. He just thought they were being nice. And now he's baking them cookies... *Because he's literally too sweet for real life.*

I must be tenser than I thought, because Jesse pulls back and peers up at me.

"Is that really necessary?" I grumble to him.

His forehead lines. "Why not?? It's a nice thing to do."

"Do you *have* to be nice to strangers?"

His lips curl at the corner. "No need to be so Grinchy, James." I narrow my gaze at him, and he chuckles. "It's Christmas. And I love baking. I want to be able to share these awesome sweets with people who will appreciate them."

I nod as he wiggles out of my arms, but not without first

pressing a soft kiss on my chest. He goes back to scooping the cookies off the baking sheet, arranging them with the others as he prepares to decorate them.

Watching him move effortlessly around the kitchen, I have this urge inside... And not the one I usually get. To cover him in icing and eat him alive.

This one is more like a fervent need to fulfill him. To give him everything he could ever desire; whatever he needs to be *happy*.

Since we moved here, we've sort of just been living vacation life, like we're retired or something. With the money I got for selling the business, we're comfortable. I know I'll need to start bringing in some money at some point, but I won't need much to finance our lives down here. More than anything, finding a job would just be something to keep me busy.

But Jesse is so young. He can't possibly just spend his time catering to me, and riding my dick until my balls are drained empty, no matter how much he loves it. He needs a project. A purpose.

Back in Maine, his plan was to take some culinary classes, and maybe start working at a restaurant. He could do that here. *But is that still what he wants?*

Jesse deserves the world. I don't want to stifle him and his potential success. I want to be the one to *give* him the world, and all the opportunities he would have had if we hadn't moved here.

Hopefully, my Christmas surprise will make that happen...

"Can I help?" I ask him, inching over, resting my chin on his shoulder and watching, captivated, while he works.

"Wanna decorate some dicks?" He grins up at me.

"Always," I hum, and he laughs.

Spinning, he hands me a bag of icing. Then he takes

another one, showing me how to use it to decorate the cookies, making them look all fancy.

I try to do one myself, muttering, "Like this?"

He pauses, his eyes flitting between the cookie and me. "That's the ugliest dick I've ever seen." He chuckles while I scowl.

"Rude." I smirk, and he elbows me. Lifting the bag, I move it up to his lips, squeezing out a dollop of white icing. He's shaking with laughter while I lean in, sucking the sweetness off his mouth. "That better?"

"Mmm... so much better," he rasps.

He licks his lips, squeezing some icing onto my nipples, and I'm cackling. Shoving me into the counter, he sighs while lapping the frosting off of me.

And, of course, the feeling wears down every bit of control I was holding on to.

Within a matter of seconds, he's up on the counter, naked, legs spread wide, with me pumping in between them.

My hips work steadily, thrusting my cock in and out of his warm, tight ass, until we're both falling apart in mutually debilitating orgasms, together. Sugar on our lips while we kiss through groans and grunts of salaciously sweet pleasure.

"I fucking love you..." he pants to me, arching up into the feelings. Up to me, because he's *mine*. "God, I love you."

"I love you so much, sweet boy. My always and forever."

Once we're cleaned up, Jesse goes back to his task, and I stay away, so as not to distract him anymore. I linger outside, on our deck overlooking the ocean, while the sun sets before my eyes. It's a tranquil vibe, lulling me into a trance.

By the time I come back inside, Jesse is done. And as ridiculous as the little cookie penises are, I'm impressed. They look awesome. Though, I'd expect nothing less. *The kid is very talented.*

"Let's go to dinner," he says on a breath, removing his apron and tossing it aside. "All the sex and baking worked up my appetite... for *food*." He smirks.

"Sounds like a plan, baby." I pat him on the butt.

We get dressed and head out to one of our favorite restaurants right on the water. We live walking distance from the resort we stayed in when we first came here for vacation last year, so we usually end up over there, at the beach and the cool spots they have for lunch or dinner.

At the restaurant, we're seated at our usual table by the waiter who loves us, Al. But when we sit down, my jaw clenches... Because I realize that the *intruders*, Blake and Kenneth, are seated at the table right next to us.

"Oh, hi!" Jesse waves at them, wearing a polite smile.

"Hey, gorgeous," Blake, the younger one, says to Jesse, standing up and kissing both of his cheeks.

It has my fist tightening by my side.

We don't know them well enough for this... *I mean, gorgeous?? Cheek kisses?? Come on.*

Blake and Kenneth seem to have a similar age gap between them that Jesse and I have. Though, if I were to guess, I'd say Kenneth is close to fifty, and Blake is probably around twenty-five.

Even so, I don't think that makes us *friends*, just because we're both gay couples with a difference in age. *Definitely not enough for them to be kissing my man...*

Kenneth does the same, and when they turn to me, I'm certainly not hiding my scowl. Jesse elbows me and I grunt, moving in closer, so they can kiss my cheeks, too. A gesture I don't reciprocate.

"I'm glad I ran into you guys!" Jesse says animatedly, picking up the container of cookies he brought along, I guess for this exact reason. "I made these for you."

Blake accepts the container, opening it up. He and Kenneth take one look inside, and burst into a cheerful shriek of laughter that grates in my ears like nails on a chalkboard.

"These are so precious!" Blake squeals.

"Gingerbread dicks." Kenneth beams. "How creative!"

Blake hugs onto Jesse, and I'm foaming at the mouth. "Thank you so much, sweetheart!"

As they pull apart, Jesse's cheeks are flushed. My jealous rage is turning up the heat inside my skin.

"I just figured... it's Christmas." Jesse rubs the back of his neck.

"A lovely gift." Kenneth touches his arm, and I'm literal seconds from ripping Jesse away from them. "So thoughtful."

"Let's push our tables together!" Blake suggests with excitement.

"I don't think—" I begin to decline, but Jesse shoots me a look that obviously says, *stop being such a grumpy hermit.*

I can almost hear him saying it.

Letting out a sigh, I fight not to roll my eyes while changing gears, mumbling, "Sure. Sounds fun."

Jesse smiles gratefully at me, sliding his fingers through mine.

For him. I'm doing this for him.

Anything to make him smile.

The guys shove our tables together while Jesse squeezes my hand, reminding me that it isn't a big deal. They're just trying to be nice...

And even if they wanted to sleep with Jesse, or both of us, that doesn't mean they get to. We spend *all* of our time alone together. What's the harm in having dinner with some new people? Just this once.

Al comes by and takes our drink order. I get a beer, but Blake and Kenneth order some elaborate tropical drinks, then aim eager gazes at Jesse, like they're expecting him to get something similar. The kid doesn't really drink... I mean, in the States, he's too young. But those rules don't apply here. Still, he's not a big drinker, and neither am I, though I like to keep a few beers in the fridge, because I genuinely like them.

"Um... I'll have the same," Jesse says, ordering what Blake and Kenneth are having, and they both cheer.

Lord, this is testing me.

I'm not sure why I'm so resistant to all of this. I don't think it has much to do with Jesse, per se. Well, I'm sure it does, in a sense, because I'm jealous and possessive as fuck. But even back home, I was a loner. I rarely ever hung out with friends.

One of the many reasons my last relationship didn't work... I hate going out and being social.

I'd much rather just be with Jesse.

And he's the same way. At least, he always *has* been. But I can't blame him for wanting to interact with other people on occasion.

So I just keep reminding myself this is good for *him*, while our drinks are delivered, and we order food.

Blake and Kenneth raise their glasses. "Here's to a tropical Christmas," Kenneth says.

"With our sexy new friends," Blake adds, winking in our direction.

I chew the inside of my cheek, following Jesse's lead, lifting my glass to clink with them.

"So... any big Christmas plans?" Kenneth asks us.

Jesse and I share a look. He bites his lip, then says, "We usually just hang out at home and exchange gifts."

I rub his shoulder lovingly. "He's being modest. He *loves* Christmas. Plans out elaborate meals and surprises..."

I give him a little grin, and he lights up. It takes away my frustrations just a tad. *I can't wait to spend our holiday anniversary with him.*

"Ooh, that sounds fun," Blake says, leaning in on the table. "So you're really just a little chef, huh?"

Jesse chuckles humbly.

"Seriously... more than just gingerbread dicks on the menu?" Kenneth asks, amused.

"Hell yea," Jesse says. "I've got a whole ass menu prepared."

Blake and Kenneth laugh, clearly impressed. *Which they should be, because he's awesome.*

"Do you work in a restaurant?" Kenneth asks Jesse.

"No," he murmurs timidly, fiddling with his glass. "No, I just like to cook..."

"Not *yet*," I cut in, and he peeks at me. "But he easily could. He could run his own restaurant if he wanted to."

Jesse stifles an illuminated smile. "Maybe someday..."

"You *will*, baby," I tell him softly, confidence lining my tone. "I fully believe you can do whatever you want. I mean, we *know* you can..."

He lets out an adorable little chuckle while giving me some major swoon eyes.

Unfortunately, I forgot we're not alone.

"Awww!" Blake cries. "That's so sweet! You two really are adorable together." He tilts his drink in my direction while speaking to Jesse. "He's so supportive of you. You're lucky." His eyes flit to Kenneth. "This one doesn't always support my passions..."

Kenneth rolls his eyes. "That's because your *passions* are creating an OnlyFans and seeking out endless partners for content."

Jesse, who was taking a sip, spits into his drink, immediately coughing hysterically as I rub his back, all the while eyeing the two dudes across the table.

I knew this was coming...

Blake argues with his partner. "Don't act like you don't enjoy the research."

The food arrives, as the perfect distraction from this increasingly awkward topic of conversation. *Not a fan of where that was going...*

As usual, the food here is delicious, so we eat joyfully while making slightly more casual small talk. The guys tell us about what they actually do, outside of recording themselves sleeping with other guys, that is. And it surprises absolutely no one to find out that Kenneth is rich.

Like, *very* rich.

"I was a broker on Wall Street," he tells us. "But after my second health scare, I decided the stress was just too much. The money wasn't worth my life. So now I spend most of my time traveling with this one." He juts his thumb in Blake's direction. "Collecting art, hosting benefits, investing... Things like that."

"Sounds fun," Jesse says with a polite smile, and I watch him closely, wondering if he thinks that's a better life than what we have here.

Does he want more? Is he... unsatisfied??

God, I hate this. I hate being in my head all the time. It's exhausting.

"Sort of similar to what you guys are doing, right?" Blake asks, looking between us. My forehead lines. "Jesse told us the other day that you're in early retirement mode right now. You sold your business and whatnot..."

I look at Jesse, and he gives me a timid smirk. *He really just told them all about our lives, huh?*

"Yea, it's a little different," I grumble. "But... sort of. I'm sure I'll need to do something else, but at least we have time to relax for a while."

The guys smile along and nod, though who knows if they're really grasping what I'm saying. I think more than anything, they're checking us out and trying to gauge whether we'd be interested in sleeping with them.

Look, I'm not saying they're *unattractive*... Sure, I've never found any man other than Jesse sexually attractive, but objectively, these two are certainly good-looking.

But still. It'll be a non-negotiable *no*. I have no interest in sharing Jesse, or myself.

I'm good, thanks.

We finish our meal, which is fantastic, as always. Then we order some coffee and dessert, which is mainly for Jesse, because dessert is his thing, and he seems like he's getting a little drunk, so the coffee might help sober him up. He's only had two of those drinks, but they're pretty much all booze. Not that he's sloppy or anything, but his face is flushed and he's been leaning on me since we finished eating.

"God," he groans with a bite of pineapple coconut cake in his mouth, eyes rolling back. "Try this."

He lifts a spoonful up to my lips and I grin, parting them so he can feed me the bite. Even if I didn't want dessert, I would never in a million years be able to resist the way he does that... And how clearly enthralled he is to do so.

"Mmm..." I rumble, leaning over his face. "Almost as sweet as you, delicious boy."

He chuckles, running his fingers up underneath my shirt while I press a kiss on his decadent mouth.

I've never been one for public displays of affection, but Jesse changes all of that. He turns me on to all kinds of new things... *Clearly.*

With his hand on my jaw, he holds me to him, kissing me deeper, sliding his tongue in to touch mine. I groan softly, reminding myself that I can't maul him right here. We have an audience.

One I don't exactly trust...

Forcing my lips off his, I clear my throat, eyes springing to Blake and Kenneth. Naturally, they're staring at us, sort of gawking, eyes glistened with intrigue.

"You're so hot together," Blake breathes. "What I wouldn't give to watch you."

My gaze narrows. I peer at Jesse and his lashes are fluttering, the way they do when he's flabbergasted.

"Watch us *what...*?" Jesse asks. I almost laugh out loud.

Come on, Jess. They're so obvious.

"Listen... I'm going to be blunt here," Kenneth speaks smoothly. "We find you both incredibly attractive. We would love to spend the night with you."

This time, I can almost *hear* Jesse's dumbfounded blinking, like the chirps of crickets.

I can't help but scoff out loud, muttering, "I knew it," under my breath.

"It can go down however you want it to," Blake adds, focusing mostly on Jesse. "We can just watch you, or we can join in..."

Kenneth leans in on the table, whispering to me, "We could trade. Just for tonight..."

Blake's hand slides across the table onto Jesse's.

Jesse's face goes from beet red to ashen in seconds flat. He yanks his hand away, mumbling, "Umm..."

But it doesn't even matter. I'm already up and out of my seat, grabbing him by the arm.

"Okay, that's enough," I grunt, pulling out my wallet and

removing some bills. "It's been fun, but I think we should be going."

"Wait wait..." Blake huffs. "Don't run off."

"No. We're going," I growl, tugging Jesse to his feet. The way he's huddled at my side, you'd think they just threatened to kidnap him. Who knows... Maybe they would have. *I don't know these assholes.* "We're not interested in sharing."

I toss my money onto the table while Kenneth stands. "Please, let me get this. I insist..."

"Not necessary." My head cocks at him. "It's not Wall Street money, but it still buys things."

Slipping my fingers through Jesse's, I yank him along by the hand, leaving the restaurant fast before that asshole can suggest putting his dick anywhere near my man again.

"Enjoy the cookies!" Jesse calls over his shoulder.

The second we're outside, I spin fast. Jesse comes crashing into me, and I grab him by the shoulders, straightening him so I can glare at his face.

"You see?" I hiss. "I *told* you..."

"You told me what??" He huffs, brows zipping together in confusion.

"This is what happens when you're *nice* to strangers," I bark. Jesse gapes at me for a moment before letting a giggle slip out. "I'm sorry... Is this *funny* to you??"

"James," he breathes, shaking his head. "You can't just assume every stranger is going to want to fuck you." He laughs. "Unfortunately, you have to give them the opportunity to hit on you so you can decline."

"I don't fucking care, Jesse," I seethe. "I could've called it from a mile away. Those dudes aren't looking for *friends*. They're looking for a sexy young toy to spit-roast on their Christmas vacation. They'd settle for me being there, but trust me, they wanted *you*. And they can't have you." I inch up to his face. "They will *never* have you."

His breathing shallows, lips parted and trembling a little as his wide golden eyes sparkle up at me.

"You're really mad...?" he whispers.

"Yes... I'm really fucking mad, Jesse." The scorch in my gaze holds his. "I'm gonna need you to not be so trusting. That those fuck-heads would even *think* they had a chance of getting near you makes me feel murderous."

And now he's blinking at *me*, cheeks flushing again, but in a different way.

There's guilt and remorse in his eyes, and it stabs at my gut just a little. I shouldn't be scolding him for being nice. Plus, it's not like he would have gone anywhere with those guys alone.

At least I hope not...

But still, I'm worked the hell up right now. *Strangers hit on my kid. My... partner.*

"I told you, I was just trying to be nice, baby..." he whines quietly, with a pout on his soft lips that's driving me insane. "I *promise*. I would never have agreed to that..."

"I know, Jess," I hum, closing my eyes for a moment while I remember to breathe, pinching the bridge of my nose. "But you were letting them ply you with booze..."

"Only because you were with me!" He gasps. "I swear to God, James, I would never..." His voice trails as he stares up at me, visibly upset now, worrying his lower lip between his teeth. "I trust you with my life. You're my guardian..." He clears his throat. "My *protector*. You always have been. Since I was a little kid, I never had to worry about feeling unsafe." He eases himself in closer to me, toying with the hem of my shirt. "As long as you're around, nothing will ever hurt me."

My heart warms at what he's saying. Of course, it's true. I

would sooner die than allow someone to harm him, or take him from me.

Reaching forward, I fold him up in my arms, crushing him to my chest while he collapses into me, burying his face in the crook of my neck. My fingers glide up his back, treasuring the feel of him as they make their way into his hair, combing through the silken locks of platinum.

"Okay, baby," I murmur. "I know. It's okay... You're right, sweet thing. I'm sorry I was upset."

He shakes his head against me. "No, I'm *sorry*. I wasn't thinking. Sometimes I just... I don't know, I get carried away wanting people to like me. Or wanting to impress them? I have no idea, but I'm sorry I scared you. I love you so much, baby."

"Please stop apologizing." I shush him, kissing his hair. "This is just me being crazy." I pull his face back with my hands, forcing him to lock eyes with mine. "And you don't need to impress anyone, or worry about them not liking you. You're fantastic, my love. Everyone who meets you loves you. Clearly..."

I grin, squinting at him while he chuckles. I watch his Adam's apple bob while he gazes at me.

"Did you really mean what you said before?" he asks. My head tilts while I touch his jaw and his neck and his shoulders. "That I can do anything... even run my own restaurant?"

I'm trying hard to stifle my knowing smirk as I nod slowly, sliding my thumb over his bottom lip.

"Sweet boy... the possibilities for someone as magnificent as you are truly endless."

His breathing picks up as he melds himself to me, grasping for my face to pull me to his mouth. In a blink, we're kissing ourselves dizzy, rough and wet and warm, spinning and spinning, standing out on the boardwalk, with people walking by... and not giving a single fuck.

Because when it comes to us, nothing else matters.

"Take me home," he whines. "Please. *Now*." His hand slides between us to cup my groin while I hum. "I need it more than I need to breathe."

A hungry snarl leaves my lips, sneaking between his. And he eats it up like his favorite treat.

"My baby's aching for Daddy?" I grip his ass hard and he squeaks, nodding fast.

"I need you to fill me up before I die," he whimpers.

Giving him a few more slow kisses, I take his hand once more, pulling him along. The walk back home is less than three minutes, but it feels like an eternity. I'm ready to combust, and the whole time we're scampering in the direction of our house, Jesse has his hands all over me.

"That was our first official fight as a couple," he whispers, while we ascend the steps to our front door.

Peeking at him, my forehead lines as I consider this. *Was it really??*

I think he's right.

I mean, I have a tendency to scold him nonstop like he's still my son. But we never actually *fight*. In fact, he seems to love when I growl things at him. It makes his dick hard.

For all the tension between us, rippling like a steady current, none of it is negative. We haven't fought about anything since we've been down here.

And even *that* just now was a pretty measly fight.

Pulling him inside the house, I close the door behind us, pressing him against it with my hips. He gasps and whines, biting his lip while I writhe into him, going for his neck.

"Does that mean we get to make up?" I nip the words onto his warm flesh.

"*Please*," he purrs, arching up to me while I work on his clothes, instantly tearing into them to get him naked. "Let me make it up to you, Daddy. Let me prove that you're the only one for me."

I almost whisper, *I know I am*. But then I stop, shuddering at the idea that he wants to be punished a little.

He wants to be my possession, and that sounds like a perfect way to end the night.

Once Jesse is in only his jeans, unbuttoned, I spin him, walking him toward the living room while sucking on his neck and feeling up all the curves of muscle in his body. He yanks my shirt off, grabbing at my chest, squeezing and squirming his dick into mine. The room is dark, minus the glow of the Christmas tree, red, green, and white lights bathing us as we move up to the couch.

Flopping down onto my back, I pull Jesse on top of me. Then I shove his jeans down over his perfect ass, my cock throbbing between us when I find what he's wearing...

A jockstrap. As in, his *whole* ass is exposed for me. *Fucking mouthwatering.*

"Look at you..." I breathe, hands sloping through all the lines of taut muscle in his torso, down to his big, thick cock, trying to burst out the front of the underwear. "You're a fantasy come to life, sweet boy."

He lets out a mewl, unbuttoning my pants with shaky fingers. I slither out of them, and he sits over my hips, straddling me while grinding slowly, rubbing our clothed cocks together until I'm leaking and burning alive.

"Get me naked, baby," I grunt, and he does, tearing my boxers off and whipping them away.

He instantly goes for my dick, like he's desperate to get it into his throat, but I stop him.

"I wanna watch you suck something else first."

He gives me a confused look while I bite my lip, reaching for the coffee table, where there's a big tray of all kinds of holiday candies. One of which being a candy cane. But not just any candy cane...

It's one of those *big* ones.

Biting open the plastic, I take it out and hold it up to him. His honey-colored eyes twinkle as he tugs his lip between his teeth.

"Show me how you suck this thick candy stick, baby," I growl, inching the peppermint cane up to his waiting lips.

He wastes no time sucking the straight end into his mouth, humming as he goes. His eyes droop while he throats it, taking it from me by the curved end, sliding it in and out of his plush pink lips.

"God, baby, you look so good," I hum, holding him by the ass, my heart thumping wildly in my chest. "Grind that big cock on me, love. Get yourself leaking inside those pretty panties."

Jesse groans with the candy in his mouth, head tipping back as he ripples his hips, riding me through his underwear, although my dick could easily slip into him, what with that open backside. But my erection is aimed up, stretching past my navel, the tip all shiny from the beads of arousal he's drawing out of me.

"Mmm..." he hums, pumping the candy cane in and out of his mouth while he grips my chest and grinds our cocks together.

My fingers slip between his cheeks. "Baby, I wanna play with this sweet hole..." Sitting fast, I slope over him, then flip his body so that his ass is before me like a feast. Covering his back with my chest, I whisper by his ear. "You sucking that peppermint good, sexy boy?"

He nods and whines, mouth stuffed full of minty candy. Spreading him apart, I suck on my finger, dragging it over his hole and watching him clench. Then I lower my mouth in between to follow its lead, licking and licking him while he pushes his hips up to my mouth.

My tongue punishes his tiny hole, slipping inside, swirling around to make him nice and wet as he arches up to me. I'm going out of my mind with need, desperate to stuff my cock into him and ride him like there's no tomorrow.

"Gimme that..." I snarl hungrily, grabbing the candy cane from him, yanking it out of his mouth.

He's breathing heavily, peering at me over his shoulder while I move the sweet, sticky candy between his cheeks.

"Are you my candy cane?" I rumble, holding him open and dragging the straight end of the minty stick over his hole.

He flinches and whines. "Yes, Daddy. *All yours.*"

"Mmm... my sweet treat..."

I continue licking him, but with the candy cane slowing teasing his ass. My tongue feathers over it, saliva dripping, the sweet minty flavor mixing with him and turning me on so bad, my balls are aching.

"*Fuck...*" he whimpers, squirming into the couch beneath us. "Stuff it in me."

My lips quirk as I lick him like a ravenous fiend, gently pushing the very tip of the candy cane into his hole.

"Such a naughty boy..." I hum, eyes locked on this salacious little game we're playing with the red and white striped confection. It nudges in just a bit, and I keep licking all the while, making sure he's nice and wet to take it in.

"Uhhfuck..." he groans, fingers digging into the cushions. "*Deeper.*"

I let a little chuckle slip. "Baby, you want this candy cane all the way inside your tight ass?"

"*Yes.*" He's literally writhing up against me, trying to get more, though I'm only giving him a couple of inches.

I'm not sure if you're supposed to put candy inside you like this... But I'll admit, even the idea of it has me pulsing out precum like no one's business.

I give him another inch, letting go and just admiring the sight of the thick candy cane sticking out of his ass.

"That is so fucking hot..." I growl, cupping his cheeks in both of my hands. "Leave it in and come suck me, baby."

Jesse lifts himself up on shaky arms, shifting a bit to face me, all the while with the candy cane in his ass like a plug. It's fucking *insane*.

But so hot that by the time his mouth is wrapped around my dick, I'm falling to pieces.

My fingers thread in his hair, gripping and holding him as he goes to town, sucking me back into his throat, swallowing and gulping until my balls are tapping on his chin.

"You're a dream come true, Jess," I mumble, looking over the slope of his back before me at the candy in his ass. "The perfect naughty little Christmas wet dream."

He moans on me, and I tug his chin to stop him before I explode down his throat. His golden eyes shimmer up at me, lips moist and trembling. Reaching behind him, I pull the candy cane out and he gasps. I toss it aside, reclining and feeling around for the bottle of lube I know is somewhere in between the couch cushions.

Jesse straddles me, and I hand him the lube, cupping his face and yanking his mouth to mine while he fumbles to open it and pour some out.

"Get us wet, baby," I breathe hoarsely into his mouth. "Make my dick nice and slippery, then ride the orgasm out of my big cock."

"God, I fucking want it," he hums, fisting my dick with a palm full of lube, stroking up and down. "I want to make you come with my ass."

"You're so good at it, sweet thing." I'm biting his lips so hard

I'm afraid I'll draw blood, but he's loving it, panting and mewling while he reaches behind himself and swipes lubrication between his cheeks.

The next thing I know, he's pushing my cock up to his hole and sitting down on me.

And I'm combusting into a thrumming ball of fire.

When his ass is on my pelvis, every inch of my dick buried inside him, he palms my chest, slowly beginning to move.

"Holy *fuuuck*..." he purrs. "My ass is all tingly from the peppermint." A breathless chuckle comes out with his words, and I can't help but huff the same.

My hands grip onto his waist. "You like fucking this candy cane even more?"

"Fuck yea," he breathes, riding me in gradual strokes, moving up and down on the rigidity of my erection. "So big and thick... God, *yesss*... so deep."

"I fucking love you, Jess..." I hum with my mind spinning and twirling, twinkling like the lights on our tree. He groans, rocking himself on me over and over, riding me roughly into the couch. "I love you more than *anything*."

"I love you," he whispers back, dropping his lips to mine once more. "You make me feel so good... Always."

As much as my loins are about to burst, so is my heart. The sex is scorching, the way he feels swallowing me up unlike anything I could even fathom. But the love we share is the truly remarkable part.

I just want this, *him*, for the rest of ever.

Jesse is bouncing on my dick, fucking me harder and faster, chasing his orgasm while our tongues tangle and we breathe each other in. I feel him tightening all over, his ass clenching and holding me as he shivers and shakes.

"You gonna come on my cock, sweet boy?" I ask, mere moments from tumbling over myself.

He nods frantically, hands everywhere, ripping at my hair, clutching my arms, playing with my nipples.

"I wanna feel it," I tell him, freeing his erection from where it's straining against the material of his jock.

Fisting, I stroke him to match him humping me wildly, riding my cock so hard the springs of our couch are creaking. His face drops to my chest, where he laps and sucks at my nipple.

"I'm gonna... *James*... Daddy, I'm... gonna—"

Before he can even finish his sentence, he lets out a harsh groan, his dick swelling up and pulsing in my hand.

His orgasm sprays all over us, on my abs and my chest, right up to where his face is. With his parted lips quivering, he catches some in his mouth, leaning down as much as he can to lick it off of me.

"*Fuck yes*, baby..." I hiss, a tremor in my nuts like an earthquake shoving me up to the edge. "Come in your own mouth. Eat up all that orgasm, sweet boy."

He grunts and gasps and moans, licking and licking until he's finally done shooting off. Then he slopes back up to my lips, kissing me fast. He pushes his tongue into my mouth, and I accept it graciously, sucking out the flavor of his cum.

"Baby, fuck me... I'm *coming*."

The climax descends over me like a monsoon, my balls pulsing, dick pouring spurts of hot cum up into his ass.

"*Fuuck, Daddy*... I feel you. I feel you coming in me," he whines, shivering in my arms, barely moving his hips any more.

He's just tightening on me, gripping my shaft and accepting every drop as I come deep inside him.

"Baby... my sweet, delicious, beautiful boy." My fingers are treasuring him, touching him sensually, our lips melting together, the sounds of us breathing ragged pants filling the room.

Hearts beating together, the way they always have. We're meant to be together, just like this.

Fuck wrong and right, fuck *anyone* who says otherwise.

"You're mine, Jess," I whisper, breathing in his scent, my lips dancing on the warm, sticky skin of his neck. "As long as I have you in my arms, my life is complete."

He lets out a sated sigh. "That's all I need."

SIXTEEN
Jesse

It's Christmas Eve. And I'm officially predictable as fuck.

Because not only am I super excited about it, but I'm also spending the entire day cooking.

I know. No one is surprised.

The thing is, though, this holiday officially means more to me than in it used to. Sure, it's always been my favorite. Something about the decorations, the lights, the presents, and the sweet goodies...

Even without the snow we used to get back home, we've still managed to turn our home into our own little tropical wonderland.

But *now*, it's more than just the most fun holiday. It's also an *anniversary*.

One year ago today, my adoptive father and I did something we most certainly were *not* supposed to do. And it changed our lives forever, which is to be expected.

It changed our lives for the better.

I don't care if other people would see it that way or not. Living down here in St. Barth has allowed us to really be ourselves. To be Jesse and James, partners in love.

I think that is definitely worth celebrating.

I decided to cook the big dinner tonight, so that tomorrow we can just eat leftovers, and spend the day relaxing. Cuddling up on the couch, or maybe out on the deck, watching the ocean.

And of course, fucking each other's brains out. *That's a given.*

Especially with the super sexy surprise gift I have for my man...

The plan is to give James his gift tonight, because I can't possibly wait until tomorrow. I have actual presents for him tomorrow, but tonight... he's gonna unwrap *me*.

While the ham and sides are roasting in oven number one, I stuff the tray of cupcakes into oven number two. Yes, our place has two ovens. It was pretty much a requirement, being I cook *that* much, certainly enough to put them both to good use.

Not that this little house had two ovens when we bought it, but James had the second one put in after we moved in. He's also done a bunch of renovations around here on his own, because he's handy. And I won't lie, watching him shirtless, hammering and drilling stuff... It pretty much guarantees me on my knees in front of him in the shower once he's done.

The brown sugar and pineapple glazed ham is baking, fingerling potatoes, carrots and parsnips with it, and a honey balsamic reduction waiting for them as soon as they're done.

I also made a tropical slaw, as a crisp, citrusy contrast. And for dessert, my famous Mexican hot chocolate cupcakes with horchata buttercream frosting.

I know what you're thinking... All of this for just the two of you? Why make so much effort?

Well, it's mainly because I just love to cook. I've always

done this. Ever since I was about sixteen and decided I loved cooking enough to think up my own recipes, I've been creating elaborate meals for James and me to enjoy as a family. Not to mention that we both love to eat, and we're sort of foodies, too.

It's fun, and it makes me happy. Cooking is like my own form of therapy.

Although right now, while I'm twirling around the kitchen in nothing but boxers and an apron covering my *May All Your Christmases Bea White* t-shirt with Bea Arthur and Betty White's faces on it, I can't help but focus on James's words from last night at dinner...

Before those two guys I thought were cool started hitting on us and he freaked out. The memory brings a little smirk to my lips.

Of course, being hit on was sort of flattering, but it's like I told James last night... Nothing ever would have come of it. Not that I'd ever yuck someone else's yum. Mad props to any couple who wants to experiment with other people in bed, safely and consensually.

But that's just not us. The thought of being with anyone other than James makes me feel yucky inside.

That said, his jealousy and possessiveness are all too delicious, and my dick swells at the memory of him, growly and mad, kissing the word *mine* onto my lips for the world to see.

In a lot of ways, I'm sure between our codependency and his jealousy, we're a few cards short of a full deck when it comes to a *healthy* relationship. But then there's so much about us as a couple that isn't *normal*. And I'm totally fine with that.

What we have works for *us*. As far as I'm concerned, nothing else matters.

What I'm really dwelling on right now is what he said about me running my own restaurant.

I can't say I haven't thought about it... Originally, before everything happened last Christmas, my plan was to take a year off after high school and figure out what I wanted to do next. As it seems, that's exactly what's happened. Only the *year* consisted of less soul-searching and researching online courses, and more being bent over and humped silly by my adoptive father.

But in the midst of all the sex and cuddling, home décor, dinners by the ocean, sunbathing and kissing and being almost annoyingly happy down here in paradise, I've had time to ruminate on plans for my future. And I think working in some sort of restaurant would make me beyond happy.

What I want is the opportunity to design my own menu, create scrumptious food and serve it to anyone who will love it. To bring people joy with my cooking.

I love cooking for only James, but I want to share my passion with others who might also devour it with enthusiasm.

I just wonder if it's even possible... And how I would go about making it happen.

"It smells *so* motherloving good in here," the rumbly voice pulls me out of my thoughts, and I peek up at the doorway where my big, sexy, muscley man is standing, in nothing but gray sweatpants—his usual attire while we're at home—dark hair tousled about, smirking at me. "My mouth is watering."

"Same." I shoot him a wicked grin and he chuckles.

Striding into the room, he makes a beeline for me, and my stomach flips and flops all crazy-like. It still happens, even a year later. He makes my knees shake, and I'm beginning to think it'll always be like this.

When he reaches me, he smooshes himself up to my back, holding me against the counter while his lips tease the sensitive flesh of my neck. I'm immediately coated in chills.

"Mmm... But this smell right here is a million times more

delicious than anything happening inside that oven," he growls, nipping me just hard enough that I flinch and purr.

"You say that now, but just wait until you've got a mouthful of pork."

He cackles out loud and my smile could probably be seen all the way back in Maine.

"I can't wait for our new tradition." He cups my ass in his hands.

My face lights up and I glance at him over my shoulder. "You mean I get more brandy-spiked eggnog?!"

He grins. "Well, sure. But I was more talking about a blowie on the couch while we watch the movies."

I chuckle and bite my lip. "I think you should blow *me* this time." He rumbles into me while I wiggle my hips. "It's only fair."

"You make a good point, sweet stuff." He nips my earlobe.

"Are you hungry?" I ask him, distracting myself from bending for him by busying my hands with combining all the ingredients for the frosting into a bowl.

"Feed me, Seymour." James does the Audrey II voice, and I laugh out loud.

"There are appetizers over there." I nod to the table across the room. "Stuffed mushrooms, a meat and cheese board... Oh, and many more gingerbread dongs. For your pleasure."

He chuckles again, giving my ass a final squeeze before untangling himself from me and practically running over to the food. I can't help but laugh, watching him eat cookies, soppressata, and gruyere at the same time.

The rest of the afternoon goes by with much of the same. James and me teasing each other, playing around, and chatting while I finish dinner and dessert. After that, we sit down to eat together, Christmas music playing in a low croon as we enjoy my scrumptious creations, making googly eyes at each other from across the table.

Once we're sufficiently stuffed, we adjourn to the living room for *A Christmas Story* and brandy-spiked eggnog. The tradition warms my chest as much as the booze in my drink. But more than that, I'm fully *obsessed* with how much better it feels being with him this way.

I'm no longer a kid with a crush, desperately trying to stuff down my illicit feelings for the man I can't have. Now, when I glance at him out of the corner of my eyes, he's already watching me. Our fingers tangled, my legs draped over his lap with his other hand on my knee. He presses his lips on my hair and I kiss his collarbone.

We stay barely dressed, touching one another subtly, tempting and tantalizing little trails of fingers and lips, my foot running up and down his calf until we're both buzzing on it.

The high of being together.

Our new Christmas Eve tradition, as a couple. *In love.*

I want to give him his gift right this second. But I have to be patient. It'll be so much better if I do it right...

He's gonna be so surprised.

"Baby..." He gives me one of his scolding tones that's actually more aroused than anything. I peer up at him. "You're wiggling all around." He grins. "Excited for something?"

"Who, me?" I bite my lip to contain the smile of an insane person. "I'm just happy to be having a perfect Christmas Eve with my man, that's all."

He narrows his gaze at me, but says nothing more, simply taking my chin in his fingers and kissing me, slow and warm and so goddamn erotic, I'm melting all over the place.

We put on another movie, watching while we snuggle up, the sun having long since dipped into the ocean outside our windows. I can't say I'm not desperate to rip off my boxers and climb onto his lap right now, but I keep reminding myself the reward will be so much better if I wait.

So the teasing touches stay that way, and eventually, we both doze off.

When I open my eyes, it's dark in the room, minus the lights from the Christmas tree. I'm reclined on my back, and James is lying on top of me with his head on my abs. I think he's drooling on me a little, which is so cute, I can't help but beam. I take a moment to comb my fingers through his mussy strands of dark hair, admiring the perfectly chiseled lines of his face, contours showing in the shadows of low light.

But then I pause. *Crap... How am I going to get out from under him??*

My mind drifts, and I remember my sleepwalking. James says I rarely do it anymore, since we moved. And I think on some level, it's definitely because of *us*. Because with him, I'm settled.

I have no reason to get up out of a bed we share together. *It's the only place I really want to be.*

Attempting to wriggle myself free, I slide out from under him, as slowly as possible, trying my absolute hardest not to wake him.

It works. But unfortunately, I fall right off the couch with a thud, shushing myself.

He's still asleep. *Thank God.*

Getting up and keeping quiet, I tiptoe over to the hall closet to get all the decorations needed for my special, sexy gift.

My eyes are on James the whole time, while I slip out of my boxers and get dressed up accordingly. I'm jittering with excitement.

I can't wait for him to see me like this. He's going to freak out...

My dick is already hard while I sneak back into the living

room. On the TV, I turn on one of those fake fireplace videos to give us some ambience.

I love it down here, sure, but at times like this, I sort of miss the fireplace. The snow falling outside while we're warm and toasty inside... It's the Christmas vibe I'm used to.

Although, we are making new traditions. *Maybe tomorrow we can do some Christmas skinny dipping in the ocean... That sounds like fun.*

Taking one final long breath to calm myself down, I sink back onto the couch by James's feet. I crawl over him, minding my *package*—LOL—and take a piece of the silver tinsel hanging around my neck, using it to tickle his chest.

I can't help but giggle quietly while I tease him. *This is so fun already. He's gonna lose his mind.*

Only a few more seconds of messing with him and he starts to shift, eyes slowly creeping open.

"What are you doing, kid..." he mumbles sleepily, grabbing me by the waist. "C'mere..."

He yanks me down, eyes closing again as he pulls me in to cuddle. Bubbles of laughter leave my lips.

"James... Goddamnit. Wake up and look at what I'm wearing."

He freezes, and his eyes reopen once more, this time taking in my ensemble. They widen.

"What the hell... is this?" He flicks at one of the bows covering my nipple.

"I'm your Christmas gift, Daddy." I smirk, cocking a brow at him. "You wanna unwrap me?"

In a flash, he's up.

Letting out a growl, he flips me onto my back, hovering over me to get a good look at my outfit. The gleam in his eyes is wickedly mischievous, gradually sliding down over the bows, the tinsel, landing on the literal wrapping paper surrounding my cock.

"Holy night..." he whispers, and I laugh. His lips curl, gray eyes flinging back up to mine. "You did this for me?"

I nod slowly. "Mhmm... You deserve a special gift, baby."

He leans down, brushing his lips over mine until I'm trembling. "You are... the most *perfect* gift I could ever receive, sweet thing."

"Prove it," I purr into his mouth. "Open me up."

This time his snarl is hungrier as he kisses me rough and possessive, sucking at my bottom lip hard, then pulling it between his teeth. I'm already squirming, my dick swelling up and threatening to burst right out of the wrapping paper. He drops his hips to it, the crinkling of the paper causing us both to chuckle while he grinds his hardening dick into mine through his sweatpants.

"Can I take my time unwrapping you, gorgeous boy?" he croons, peppering my jaw with kisses that move down to my throat.

"You can tease and torment me all you want, Daddy. I'm your gift to play with."

James hums, licking and sucking down my neck, minding the silver tinsel I have wrapped around it, nibbling at my collarbone before moving on to my chest.

Covering my nipples are a green and a red bow. His eyes lock on mine as he slides his finger between them, running it down my abs to my navel. Around my waist, there's a string of something I made...

His eyebrow arches, and I hum, "That's mistletoe, you know..."

He bites his lip. "Is it now?"

I nod, and he lets out a growly sound, lowering his mouth to my chest this time. He kisses all over me, but doesn't remove the bows, licking the lines of my pecs, then making a trail through my abs to where the string of mistletoe is around my waist. He nips and nuzzles in my happy trail, and I'm just *dying*.

I'm already keyed up so tight, my dick hard and pushing against the candy cane wrapping paper around it.

It's kind of hilarious that the paper is decorated with candy canes... after what happened last night.

Guess it was meant to be.

James is eyeing my dick, meticulously wrapped up in paper with a smaller silver bow atop my shaft. It's moving in there as it grows and swells, becoming engorged from his teasing touch and just the way he's staring at it.

I tug my lip between my teeth as his fingers gently brush along the paper. I gasp, and his gaze springs briefly to mine.

"This is a *big* present..." he rumbles, casually touching me, fingertips grazing down to my balls. Another soft sound leaves me, my eyes observing the way his broad chest is fluttering with heavy breaths, the outline of his thick cock showing itself from within his pants. "I can't wait to unwrap it."

Then he slowly tears into the paper, freeing my cock. It's already hard as stone, sort of bursting out as he whips the paper off to the side, humming and settling in between my legs.

"It's just what I wanted." He grins up at me, and I chuckle. "How did you know?"

"I took a guess." My tongue touches to my top teeth.

"And the mistletoe..." He runs his hands up and down my thighs, massaging them as he goes. It feels so good, my eyelids are drooping. "Right above it. I guess that means I'm supposed to *kiss*..."

I'm watching in eager fascination as his mouth lowers to the head of my dick, pressing a soft kiss on the fleshy crown. I can't help but whimper, and he does it again, slower this time, kissing the tip of my cock sensually, the way he kisses my lips.

His tongue extends as he does, fluttering the underside of my head, on that sensitive spot that makes my entire cock move. He grins wide.

"I think he likes that…"

I gulp, burning up and panting. "He definitely does."

He keeps going, kissing and licking at the end of my dick, so slowly and so thoroughly, I'm going out of my fucking mind. His soft lips part, my dick pushing between them as he sucks gently, pulling out pulses of arousal.

"Mmm… so *delicious* already," he growls, his voice vibrating into me.

With his hands on my hips, he sucks me in deeper, but only by an inch, really working his tongue, cradling my cock with it while his hips ripple into the couch, clearly grinding out some much-needed friction on his own erection.

"Jesus… your mouth…" I whine, reaching for his hair.

My fingers comb through the silky dark strands, subtly attempting to push his warm, wet mouth farther down on my aching cock.

But he pauses, grabbing my hands quickly and pinning them down at my sides.

"*My* gift," he murmurs in a hoarse rumble. "I get to play with you however I see fit."

"Yes, Daddy…" I whimper, and he groans.

His mouth picks up in leisurely sucks, the warmth, the softness of his lips and his tongue, the dedication in the gradual waves of him taking me in… It's all winding me up like crazy. I'm burning so hot with need, I can't even help but push my hips upward, trying to fuck into his sweet mouth as much as I can.

Because James's mouth is my ultimate gift. It's something I

never expected I could have before last year... And the first time he ever wrapped his pink lips around my dick, I was sure I had died and gone to forbidden heaven.

I still feel that way every single time he sucks me. Especially when he does it the way he's doing it right now... As if he's purposely trying to torture me with euphoric pleasure.

My balls are drawn up so tight already, it feels like he's squeezing them in his hand.

Oh wait, he is.

James has his index finger and thumb curled around my nuts, squeezing and tugging them while he sucks my cock, the sting of pain turning me on *so* much more. With every bead of precum dripping from my tip, his tongue lashes over it, licking up the flavor as he sucks me back into his throat.

"Fffuck... fuck yes... *James.*" I'm rambling out words, barely even aware of what I'm saying as I arch up to his hungry mouth. "You suck me so good, Daddy. I fucking *love* it..."

He hums on my dick, pulling his mouth away to take a deep breath. "I have an idea."

Fuck me. I love the sound of that even more.

Suddenly, he's up, ripping off his sweatpants to reveal all the immaculate inches of his huge cock. When he comes back to me, he straddles my shoulders backwards, immediately dropping his mouth back down onto my dick.

My shaky hands cup his ass, a thrill moving through me like electricity. *Fuck yes. I love sixty-nine time.*

James falls back into sucking me upside down, stuffing me all the way back into his throat while I whimper and purr, licking a line up his shaft to his balls. Nuzzling them with my lips, I lap at them like a delicious treat before sucking them gently into my mouth.

James groans on my cock, and I groan back, loving the good

feelings I'm giving him while he gives me mine. *This is why sixty-nine is awesome...*

There's something about pleasuring him with my mouth at the same time he's pleasuring me with his. It's like a seesaw. Tit for tat.

A game of HORSE, where each lick, suck, and nip from him is returned and expanded on.

Only this time, I'm going in for a different feast.

Angling James's cock into my mouth, I give him a few generous sucks, before moving back up to his balls. And then, I spread his ass open with my hands, licking a warm line up his taint... To his yummy little virgin ass.

I mean, I have to *assume* his ass is a virgin, because we've never done anything with it. James is a top for sure, and I'm undoubtedly a bottom. I think it's safe to say if he were interested in even just a finger inside him here and there, we would've done it by now.

I'm definitely not trying to get inside his ass, unless he wants me to. I'd do literally anything for him, but I love our sexual dynamic the way it is. That said, everyone deserves to have their ass eaten. *It's just a fact.*

I can feel James tense with my mouth in between his cheeks. It has a devious grin on my lips as I press a slow kiss on his hole, giving it a little licky lick.

A jagged moan rumbles onto my dick. It lights a fire inside me...

He likes it. This is awesome... God, I wanna eat the fuck out of his ass.

Why have we never done this before??

Going for broke, I give him my whole tongue, feathering it over his tight hole, licking and licking while kissing and sucking, using my entire mouth to worship him. My fingers are digging into his ass, gripping and squeezing onto him hard while I devour him like he's my last meal.

He pops off my dick, dropping his cheek onto my thigh while pushing his hips back against my mouth. "*Fffuck...* Jess. That feels so fucking good..."

"Ride my face," I growl, pulling him closer. *Who needs to breathe anyway?*

I stuff my tongue inside him, and he shudders.

"*Jesus...* Jesus fucking Christ..." He grips my thigh, fisting my cock in his other hand and stroking me while swiveling his hips over my mouth. "Eat me... *fuck*, eat me alive."

Groaning into his ass, I reach around and grab his cock, jerking him the way he's jerking me, all the while using my lips and tongue on him, making a sloppy mess and not giving a single fuck.

James's dick is engorged. I can practically feel it throbbing in my palm as he chases the good feelings, humping my fist and rocking back to ride my tongue.

This is so insanely dirty and filthy and spectacular. I think I could come just like this...

I think I might. Like, soon.

But of course, James stops it... The edging he always manages to inflict on me, which I'm sure is intentional. He whips himself off me, flipping around and coming back to kneel in between my legs.

"I'm gonna fuck you so fucking hard, you beautiful, sexy, perfect thing," he growls, pushing my legs apart as wide as they'll go.

He feels around in the couch, frantically searching for the lube.

"Just spit on me and go in raw," I plead, chest pumping like my pulse, the sounds of us breathing heavily echoing off the walls.

"Oh no..." he mumbles, hovering over me. "I'm gonna need you nice and slippery wet for what I'm about to do to you."

His dark eyes fall to my lips, and he bites his. I can tell he wants to kiss me, so I reach up and grab his jaw, yanking him down to my mouth.

"Your ass is fucking delicious, Daddy," I whisper, kissing him furiously, licking and sucking on his lips. "Taste it."

And of course he gives right in, returning it, biting me and sucking my tongue into his mouth. A shivering groan slips between my lips and I swallow it up, clutching onto the thick muscles in his chest, lifting my hips to rub my ass on his dick.

"Get the fucking lube, please," he begs, raspy and overflowing with need. "I think it's under you somewhere..."

Nodding fast, I reach beneath the pillow behind my head, finally locating the tube. He snatches it, pouring out a generous amount of lubrication while our mouths maul one another, kissing so hard my lips are already swollen.

James coats himself, swiping slick fingers over my hole. He stuffs one inside and I whine, eyes falling shut instantly.

I have never craved being stuffed full the way I do with James. It's like my body physically *needs* him. Like I'm missing one very important piece until he clicks it into place.

"Jesse..." he whispers my name, withdrawing the finger and replacing it with his cock.

"J-James..." I quiver out, relaxing myself for a forceful thrust I know is coming.

But instead of shoving his dick inside me, he pushes it *slowly*, gently, easing himself into my ass while his lashes flutter and he moans on a quiet breath, "I... love... *only*... you."

Chills sheet my flesh as I welcome him inside me, my body gripping every inch of his cock until his pelvis is on my cheeks. My lips are shivering, eyes rolling back at the sensation of him, warm and hard, claiming my body with his.

Owning me, because he does.

It feels like this is my purpose. *I'm meant to be his, forever.*

"Baby, open your eyes," he hums, holding my face with our bodies zipped up. "Look at me, beautiful. Let me watch you while I fuck what's mine."

"*Yours...*" I croak, gazing up at him through hazy vision. "Only yours, James."

He lays a sweet kiss on my lips, pulling back just enough so that our eyes are locked while he begins to move, drawing his hips back, then thrusting into me. Deep... He's so *deep*, all the way in me, with my balls resting on his warm skin.

James is fucking me slowly, sensually, moving in and out at a pace that truly feels like we're making love, shaky gasps and groans and cries leaving our lips in tandem. We're melded together, his hot, muscled body draped over mine, rubbing against my cock with every movement. It feels *sublime*.

"God, I love how you fuck me..." I whimper.

"Yea?" His pace picks up, but not by much. He's still just pumping between my legs, his cock riding my prostate so good I'm seeing stars.

"Yes..." I gasp, legs curled around his waist, ankles locked atop his perfect ass.

"You love the feeling of my big cock in your warm, tight little ass?" He reaches for the tinsel around my neck, gripping it tight.

A quaking sound flees my lips. "Yea... Mmmfff... big... uhh cock."

"This is how you like to be played with, huh, sweet gift?" He moves back enough to run his free hand down my body, sort of choking me with the tinsel. "You love me, rock hard and fucking you as deep as possible?"

"Yesss..." My eyes roll back when he rips the bows off my nipples, dropping his mouth to my chest.

He licks my nipple, swirling his tongue around and around it, before doing the same to the other, sliding his cock in and out of me steadily.

"Yes...?" He bites me and I flinch.

"*Daddy...*" I sob, his cock sending lightning bolts through my loins. "Fuck me *deep* with that rock-hard dick, Daddy."

James growls out a noise that's a little uneven, one which tells me he's getting close. Releasing the tinsel, his hands caress me all over, down to my hips, then onto my thighs. He moves my legs, lifting them so my ankles are up by his ears while he fucks into me harder and harder, really riding my ass deep.

I'm moments from exploding. I can feel it winding up like a rubber band. The way his huge cock is brushing my spot, the sight of him, glistening in a sheen of sweat, illuminated by the glow of the Christmas tree's lights, black strands of hair hanging in his face, full lip being tugged by his teeth.

God, I'm going to erupt... This man is a sex machine. I can't... hold...

"I wanna..." James rasps, lifting my hips even more, rocking his dick into me while lowering his mouth. "I want... *Jesse, baby...* I just want... to..."

And then he extends his tongue, feathering it over my dick.

My dick literally lurches upward, like it's trying to jump into his mouth. He's holding my hips up as high as he can get them, while still connected to me, his dick stroking in my ass in shallow pumps.

He grabs my cock in his hand, aiming it up to his lips. And he sucks on the head, like a lollipop, while fucking me.

"Mmm... mm mm... mmmm," he groans out noises, sucking on me desperately while stuffing my ass with cock, and it's just... too much.

I can't...

"I'm gonna..." I gasp, and before I can even get the next word out, I come.

I come almost *viciously*, the orgasm racking through me, pulses of cum shooting into James's mouth while he whimpers and swallows them back.

His hips never stop moving. He keeps gliding his cock in and out of me while I buzz and contract, crying out all kinds of nonsense with my eyes rolling back in my skull.

"Coming... so hard. Best... orgasm... *holy fuck*. I love you... James... *Daddy*... Fuck fuck fuck me."

James slurps out every last drop of my cum, releasing my dick with a pop from his lips and setting my hips back down. And then he turns feral.

He grinds himself into me, driving deeper and deeper, fucking the life out of me until the whole couch is skidding along the floor.

His forehead falls to mine, and he whispers, "I'm gonna come so deep in you, baby."

That's it. *Famous last words.*

He collapses onto me, crushing me with his body weight as he grunts and groans, the feeling of his dick shooting cum off deep inside my body, causing me to leak out even more. His hands are in my hair, on my face, his lips kissing my neck in between gasps of a very intense orgasm.

His body is singing for me.

I love it so damn much.

His hips move gradually, stuffing every last drop into me, and he lets out a ragged breath.

"That was... insane," he sighs, fingertips trailing up and down over every reachable surface of my sticky skin.

"Yea, it was," I hum, touching him back. His chest, shoulders, arms. I can't get enough.

I want to stay like this forever.

Lifting himself up, he rests his chin on my chest, gazing up at me with his gray irises twinkling. I truly love the look of him like this... All flushed and sexed up. Sweet and sated and in love.

It's probably my favorite look of his.

"Jess..." he murmurs, brushing my hair back with his fingers. "You are so hypnotizing, baby."

I can't help but gulp, emotions welling up that are kind of strange. I'm not one to get emotional after sex, but I guess sometimes you really just feel it; the connection. The *love*.

"I mean it," he keeps going. "You're *gorgeous*... stunning, really. Smart, and funny, and talented. Caring and loyal, dedicated and kind... You're just *perfect*, baby. There has never been, nor will there ever be, someone as wholly fantastic as you." I blink at him, tears pushing behind my eyes that make me feel kind of foolish. But I can't help it. "I'm the luckiest man alive, being able to know you... To *have* you."

"James..." I whimper, touching his chest, trying to stifle some of this heaviness. His heart is thumping wildly beneath my hand.

"Jess, just listen..." He adjusts his hips and I whimper at the feeling of him, still inside me. He lets out a soft sound. "I want to have you forever..."

He pulls out of me, drawing out a gasp. Then he takes my hand and tugs me until I'm sitting up, my head spinning as the sensation of his cum dripping out of me flushes my cheeks.

"I want to *hold* you... forever," he says, his eyes wider than they were a moment ago. "I want to comfort you and care for you... I want to support you, and cherish you. I want only *you*... always."

He stops to swallow visibly, sliding off the couch. Onto his knees.

"What are you... doing..." I whisper, lashes fluttering like crazy while my heart leaps in my chest. *What's happening right now...?*

"I want you... in sickness and in health." He ignores me and goes on, holding my hand in his, kneeling on the floor before me. "In good times and bad. I want you to be my partner for the rest of our lives, Jesse. I want you in every way I could have you... and I just hope that you want the same. Which is why, *right now...* I want to ask you..."

"Holy crap, I'm gonna faint..." I gasp, and he laughs.

"Baby... Will you marry me?"

My heart has come to a complete stop.

Time is no longer moving... We're suspended. And I'm just staring down at him, this man who used to be my father, and who is now *so* much more...

Kneeling on the floor and asking me to be his husband?!

It's crazy. Completely ridiculous, the most terrifying and incredible thing I've ever heard anyone say.

But there's only one response. There is only one word I could use to answer a question like this...

"Yes," I croak, with tears immediately flowing down my cheeks. I couldn't stop them if I wanted to. "Yes... Fuck yea, of course I'll marry you."

I launch myself at him.

My heart is soaring behind my ribcage, adrenaline making me all twitchy, my mind running a mile a minute. I'm only ninety percent sure this is actually happening.

But if it is a dream, I never want to wake up.

The man of my dreams just asked me to marry him...

And I said yes.

Holy fuck, we're engaged!

James is chuckling, all sweet and sexy and nervous while I tackle him to the floor, kissing his neck and face, everywhere my lips can reach. I've completely forgotten for a moment that we're naked, until I feel his dick twitching on my abs.

"Baby..." I sniffle, lifting to look down at him. "You really just proposed to me...?"

He beams, the smile of someone so desperately, almost stupidly in love, covering his face.

Okay, I lied. This is my favorite look on him.

"I did," he hums, holding my face. "And you said yes."

I bite my lip. "We're gonna get married...?"

He nods. "Yea. We are."

"Fuck..." I whimper, dropping my face back into his neck so he doesn't see me cry like a total loser.

"We might need to wash out that mouth of yours with soap, kid," he teases.

"Yea, probably," I grumble to cover up the shake in my voice. "It's done some pretty filthy things."

He laughs out loud, lifting me up and forcing me to look at him. "I'm sorry..."

My brow furrows. "For what?? In case you can't tell, I'm ecstatic."

He grins. "No... it's just... I didn't plan on asking you like this. While we're naked and sweaty... post-stupefying orgasm."

I chuckle. "Were you carried away by the moment...?"

He nods. "Yes. Very much."

I drop a kiss on his lips. But then I pause. "Wait, so you've been planning this?" His eyes sparkle up at me and he bites his lip. "You've been... *wanting* to ask me?"

"Jess," he hums, thumb grazing my lower lip. "*Of course* I have. Being here with you... living this life, this dream... It's everything I never thought I'd have. Being truly in love and happy... I didn't think it was in the cards for me. I never thought I'd... want to marry someone." He stops to breathe out slowly.

"But *you*... You're a dream come true, baby. Marrying you would be as easy as breathing."

I pout, fighting tooth and nail against the tears of joy that want to keep flowing from my eyes.

"Well, you already know..." I huff, steadying my trembling words. "I've dreamed of you falling in love with me since before I even really knew what it meant. I didn't think having *you* the way I wanted was in the cards... So now that it is..." My forehead lowers to his. "Marrying you is *my* dream come true."

His hands cup my face, and he kisses me, slowly, full of passion; a dedication, an unexpected devotion.

It's the same way he's been kissing me for the last year. One whole year, Christmas to Christmas... And here we are.

It started as a mistake we were never supposed to make... and it turned into happily ever after.

With his question, we've wiped away the past, the history, and everything holding us back.

We're no longer a father and his adoptive son. We're engaged.

We're going to be *husbands*.

We have a future, together. The perfect gift for us to unwrap.

EPILOGUE
James

Waking up this Christmas feels different in a lot of ways.

For one, it's sunny outside. And warm. Missing the snow we're used to back home. But that won't be a problem for long... *Since I have a couple more surprises up my sleeve.*

That's the other reason why this Christmas feels different. Because on *this* holiday morning, when our eyes peel open, and we look at each other... We're already smiling.

Because we're *engaged*.

"Good morning, fiancé," Jesse murmurs sleepily, stretching his arms over his head.

"Good morning to *you*, fiancé." I kiss his pulse. "Merry Christmas."

"Merry Christmas, baby."

We ended up falling asleep on the couch again after the unexpected proposal, which is actually good for my next surprise.

It means I get to see my fiancé's face light up, which is so thrilling I can't seem to stop my toes from wiggling.

The thing about proposing to Jesse is that I'd been thinking about it for a while. I've known, pretty much since the moment we got together, that I wanted to marry him. But I couldn't help myself from getting hung up on making the proposal itself as memorable as possible.

I almost did it on his birthday, back in August. But I chickened out and wound up making him come four times instead. *Either way, I think he had a great night.*

But last night, after that soul-cleansing orgasm, and the way he was looking up at me, rosy cheeks, tousled platinum hair, eyes the color of golden treasures... I found that I just couldn't help myself.

I couldn't wait one more minute to become his fiancé. Fortunately for me, he said *yes*. And we spent the rest of the night kissing and touching on the couch, being deliriously happy, for the best Christmas Eve ever.

"I really need to shower," Jesse grumbles, sitting up, wincing over what I'm guessing is muscle strain from the wild sex last night. "And because I'm so sore, I'm looking for volunteers to wash me. Maybe a certain... fiancé is up to the task?"

He grins at me, and I chuckle, kissing a line down his bicep. "That *absolutely* sounds like something I could manage."

The two of us finally stand up on wobbly legs and race through the house toward our bedroom. The master bath is attached, meaning you have to go through the bedroom to get to it. Which also means that as soon as Jesse is pushing the door open, I'm jittering with excitement.

As soon as it's open, and he looks inside, his face freezes. His mouth is open, eyes wide. Just pure shock and awe, and I'm living for it.

"Merry Christmas," I sing to him by his ear.

He gasps out a laugh of disbelief, then peeks at me. "You did this??"

"No, some other awesome fiancé broke in and decorated

the bedroom like a winter wonderland." I roll my eyes teasingly, and he shoves me.

"I can't even believe what I'm seeing!" He cheers, prancing into the room.

There's fake snow everywhere. Lights and decorations strewn up on the walls of our bedroom, two more smaller Christmas trees, a fake fireplace... Even our bedding is different. It's all flannel red and green, covered in a fuzzy throw. The whole room looks like back home, in the northeast.

"I thought... just in case you missed being in Maine for Christmas," I tell him, walking up behind him and wrapping my arms around his waist. "I'd bring Maine to us."

He gazes up at me. "You're amazing. I love you so much."

Pushing up to my lips, he kisses me softly, which of course turns heated, because we're both still naked.

We end up pawing at each other, shoving one another toward the shower, where I fuck him until we both come, and then we wash each other up, slow and cherishing. *A new Christmas morning tradition.*

Once we're *finally* clothed again, Jesse shouts, "Time for presents!" and darts out of the room.

Chuckling, I shake my head, following after him. But apparently, I'm not moving fast enough, because he starts barking at me from up the hall.

"Hurry up! Come on come on come *on!*"

"Alright... Jesus," I grumble. "Hold your reindeer."

But when I get to the living room, he's not there. He pokes his head around the corner from the hall. "Your big gift is outside."

Okay, now I'm intrigued.

I follow him, or rather, allow him to drag me by the hand, outside onto the back deck. He brings me down to our little yard area, then stops, grinning at a pile of stuff on the ground.

"Tada! Merry Christmas," he says while bouncing around animatedly.

"Thanks, baby..." I hum, cocking my head. "What, uh... is it?"

He jaunts over to the pile. "It's everything we'll need to start our own garden. Or rather, *your* garden."

He beams at me, and I'm speechless. I'm just blinking at his beautiful, cheerful face, my heart swelling up behind my ribs.

He's giving me a garden...?

"See, all of this wood we'll use to build the fence. There's chicken wire, and rope, and everything you need." He smiles at me. "I know you miss being able to grow things... And now you can. You can grow whatever you want here. Well, whatever the weather will permit. But, spoiler alert, I also got you some stuff for indoor growing in the den. It's not like we use it anyway."

"Baby..." My head shakes back and forth as I stomp over to him, taking his face in my hands. "This is such an incredible gift. Thank you so much."

"And the best part is that we get to do it together." He grins. "We've got nothing but time, and I figured this would be a fun thing for us to do. As partners. Or fiancés. Or *husbands*." He bites his lip, and I laugh.

"Well... to be fair, you might not have as much free time on your hands as you think..." My fingers trail his jaw, and his forehead lines. I show him a wicked smirk, nodding toward the house. "Come here, baby. Let me give you your gift."

He looks nervously excited, just like he did last night when I was about to propose, and I swear, it's the best possible look on him. Taking him by the hand, I drag him back into the house, to the living room.

Picking up a flat box wrapped in snowman paper, I hand it to him, unable to stop from fidgeting in place. He rips it open like a wild animal, confusion gracing his features when he finds the documents and a set of keys.

"What is this...?" he asks, looking everything over, his eyes bugging out of his head.

"Congratulations, Jess," I whisper. "You're the new owner of your very own shop down on Main Street."

He's stunned speechless for a few seconds, before he mutters, "Do you mean that empty space where the coffee shop used to be?" His eyes spring up to mine.

I nod. "Yup. It belongs to you."

"Oh my God..." He gasps, his face immediately morphing into one of mesmerized elation. "Oh my God! I can't believe you did this!"

He tosses the box onto the couch and attacks me, leaping up into my arms. I catch him by the butt, hugging onto him tightly while he kisses my lips over and over.

"I get to open my own restaurant," he whimpers, emotions clearly bubbling over. I can't help but feel them too. *Making him this happy is like taking a unicorn ride over a rainbow.* "Holy crap, it's really happening. I get to open my own place! Design my own menu, choose ingredients... I get to cook for a *living!*"

He squeals, and I laugh, running my fingers up and down his back. "Yea, you do, baby. You get to run the show."

He pulls back to blink up at me. "Are you sure I can do it...?"

"Is that a serious question?" I ask, my lips curving.

He squeals again. "Who am I kidding? Of course, I can do it! This is my dream!"

"Yea, it is, baby," I chuckle, kissing his bottom lip.

"And you made it happen..." He sighs with hearts in his eyes. For *me*. "James... I just..." He shakes his head. "Between the proposal and now this... You're rocking my world this

Christmas, baby." He kisses my smile. "I can't believe you did this for me..."

"It's not just for you, baby," I tell him, thumbs drawing circles on his jaw. "It's for *us*. This is our future. Getting married, starting a business... Starting a life. It's all I want... With you, Jess."

"I can't wait to build a life with you," he whispers on my mouth.

Our kisses slow down. And we feel it; the excitement of so many wonderful new things happening in our world.

I think him giving me a garden is fitting... Because of everything we'll be growing together. A business, a marriage. A relationship that means something, not just a hidden affair.

With this man in my arms, I'll want for nothing else.

He's it. The gift of a lifetime.

Jesse

Four Months Later

"Am I dead??"

I have to laugh at that. Leaning over the counter, hands clasped together, my grin is uncontrollable while I watch James devouring all the little sample items on the plate.

"No, I'm serious," he grumbles once he's swallowed the mouthful of pineapple macadamia shortbread. "I think I've died and gone to heaven, because this food, baby... It tastes like it was baked by an angel."

I bite my lip. "You're way too good for my ego. Let's just hope the food critic dude shares your enthusiasm."

"I know he will." James grins, reaching over and grasping the top of my apron, yanking me forward to press a soft kiss on my lips. "I mean... He doesn't need to share *all* the enthusiasms I have for you..."

Chuckling, I flick my tongue over his lower lip. "Well, it wouldn't be the worst thing for him to think I'm hot. It could help my cause."

James scowls at me, and I laugh even harder.

We're spending the afternoon here. I'm designing a special tasting for a food critic who's going to come in tomorrow and taste my stuff. Hopefully, he ends up loving it, and writes a glowing review in the local paper that will drive business for the grand opening, which is happening in one week.

To say I'm nervous would be a bit of an understatement, which is why it's a good thing James is here today, giving me that confidence boost I need. I can always count on him as my cheerleader.

Sometimes I like to picture him in a short skirt with pom-poms. It makes me laugh to myself.

Together, we've spent the last four months getting the business together and ready to open. J&J Café is everything I ever dreamt it could be. I designed it all myself, from the interior décor to the appliances, and obviously the menu, which I'll be changing up regularly. And James helped me make it a reality.

He's been handling the business side, though by no means has he taken it over. Mainly, he's just helping me learn about it, sort of like a silent partner. And I have to appreciate the hell out of him for that. Because business has never really been my forte. But it comes easily to James, since he ran his own business for years. A successful one, at that. He could easily just take the reins, but instead, he's patient and supportive.

He's actually a really good teacher. *Just one of his many talents.*

He also helped me hire my staff. Six servers for a rotating schedule, a sous chef, and two additional cooks to help me and make it so I don't have to work all day every day, and just a few more people for cleaning and whatnot. It's crazy to think I have people working for me... *And I'm not even twenty years old yet!*

But I believe I can do this. And with James's help, we can't lose. *We make a great team... We always have.*

On top of all the exciting things happening with the café, James is going full speed ahead with his garden. The dude has a very green thumb.

It's been so successful in yielding fruit and some vegetables, we'll actually be using a lot of the produce in our cooking at the café. *Talk about fresh ingredients.*

I'm just loving life right now. Living the dream here in our tropical slice of heaven.

"Okay, so which was your favorite, from each course?" I ask James, pencil in hand, ready to jot down some more notes.

I need to make sure I'm choosing the best options for the tasting.

James gives me his list of favorites, and I have to agree with him on most of them. We spend the next hour finalizing it, and I give the list to Sean, my sous chef, who's going to prep everything.

By the time we're done, the sun is setting, and James and I head outside, bidding farewell to my home away from home for the night.

Our place is walking distance from the café. It's fully amazing. It's ten minutes on foot, but still. The weather right now is perfect, and our favorite thing is to walk around with the ocean breeze brushing our skin, holding hands while we chat and decompress from the day.

Once over the bridge, with our house in sight, James tugs

me down a side street, and I give him a peculiar look. "Where are we going?"

He has a mysterious little smirk resting on his lips as he hums, "You'll see."

This man is full of surprises... It could be stressful, if he weren't so awesome at making all of my dreams come true.

The quiet street leads us down to the water, a few yards from our little stretch of beach. James brings me along a path, to an inlet. It's a purely stunning sight.

Tropical plants and flowers everywhere, the tranquil sound of the water. Beneath some trees, he stops me, holding my hands in his. He faces me, biting his lip with his stormy eyes resting on mine.

"What do you think?" His brow cocks.

My gaze moves around us, and then I blink up at him. "For what?"

"Do you like this spot?" He ignores my question, asking his own.

"Yea," I huff through an obvious grin. "It's beautiful. Aren't we on someone's property, though?"

He chuckles. "This is town property. This little spot right here, beneath these trees... I think it's the perfect place."

I swallow hard. "Perfect place... for what?"

"For us to get married." He beams.

My heart is immediately racing. We haven't talked much about our actual marriage ceremony in the last four months. We've been pretty preoccupied with getting the café ready. And really, we've just been enjoying being engaged.

It's not like we have to worry about inviting people to a big wedding, or having a fancy ceremony. We both agreed it makes the most sense for it to just be us. Maybe even have a small reception party thing at the café afterward, with the staff, who are now my friends...

I think it could be fun.

But still, it's all been just talk... Until now.

Now, he's standing here, eagerly gazing at me, awaiting my confirmation about this spot... As the location for our wedding.

I'm floored. But excited. Actually, I'm brimming with anticipation.

And I think it shows, because James chuckles and grabs my face, brushing his soft lips over mine.

"Do you love it?" he whispers, and I nod.

"I love it," I rasp.

"Do you want to get married right here?" he asks, sealing our bodies together while the ocean breeze rustles our hair.

"I do." I grin wide, and he laughs some more.

"Good. Meet me here this Saturday evening." He presses a kiss on my mouth, but my head is spinning.

"This Saturday??" I gasp. "As in... *three days* from now??"

He nods with confidence. "Mhm. As long as you say yes, baby... I can't wait to marry you this Saturday, right here in this beautiful spot."

My eyes creep open and I stare at him, admiring the hell out of this amazing man... The man who raised me, who brought me up, who taught me everything I need to know about life and the world...

Who will spend the rest of our lives teaching me, and loving me, and supporting me...

Being my *husband*.

"I want you to open that café married to me," he says, his deep rumbling voice packed to the brim with so much love and devotion, it almost brings tears to my eyes. "I want us to move into this next phase of our lives... betrothed."

I cackle out loud. "*Betrothed?* I've literally never heard you say that word."

His smile is brighter than the moon over the sea. "I never had a reason to say it before."

Biting on the inside of my cheek, I nod. Fast and frantically. "Yes. I can't wait to marry you... right here. On Saturday. I can't wait to dive headfirst into this awesome life with you, James McCallister."

He lifts my left hand, kissing my finger. "I can wait to put my ring on you."

"You'll be stuck with me..." I smirk, and he kisses it.

"I've been stuck with you since you were two years old, Jesse." He chuckles, and I squint at him. "The best thing that ever happened to me."

I nod. Because he's right.

From the sadness, and the devastation, we were able to make joy. Out of the forbidden, we found forever.

The End.

Acknowledgments

Thank you so much to everyone who made this sweet, sexy, forbidden little novella possible!

To Sara Cate, and the entire crew from the *Twisted Christmas Anthology*! I'm so glad we decided to bring these taboo stories to life!

To Kenzie of Nice Girl Naughty Edits for being my proofreading baddie, my graphic queen. Girl, you deserve a few gingerbread dongs for being so amazing!

To Nisha's Books & Coffee PR for handling the release of my holiday novella. You're awesome, and I have to thank you for all of your hard work on rocking this one with me!

Cady & Tori from Cruel Ink Editing and Design, who did the cover and the interior formatting... I'm so happy to be working with you lovely baddies on this! You made this package something yummy to unwrap ;)

Anyone who read Jesse and James last year as a part of the anthology, you guys rule! I'm so grateful to all the awesome readers who enjoyed these two dudes and their forbidden love story.

To the Flipping Hot Fandom... You are my ride or dies. I can never tell you how important you are to me... How much having you by my side gives me peace in the craziness of my mind. I love you all!

And to all of the Nyla K readers, the fans of unique and smutty weirdness I provide... You are the best thing in my world. Thank you for believing in me, loving my stories, my characters, and the deep love they possess. I can't wait to keep giving you all the gifts I have to offer.

Other Works

Thank you for reading
Flipping Hot Fiction by Nyla K

Subscribe to my Patreon for bonus content, like *The Vacation* (PUSH/Alabaster Pen, etc. Crossover), and more!

The Midnight City Series:

Andrew & Tessa's Trilogy
(MF Forbidden/Age Gap, celebrity romance, suspense. Read in order)
Midnight City (TMCS #1)
Never Let Me Go (TMCS #2)
Always Yours (TMCS #3)

Alex & Noah
Seek Me (TMCS #4 – Standalone/Spin-off, MF, Friends to lovers/Angst)

**Unexpected Forbidden Romance:**

PUSH (Standalone, Taboo/MMF, bi-awakening)
PULL (Continuation novella!)
Trouble (Spinoff, MM, gay-awakening, second chance)
Audio for the Love Is Love books available now!
To Burn In Brutal Rapture (Standalone, MF, Taboo/Age Gap)
Double-edged (Standalone, MMM Age Gap, Twincest – **BANNED by Amazon!** Can be found on Nyla's website, Google Play & Eden Books.)
For The Fans (Standalone, MM, Stepbrothers)
Also available in audio!

**Alabaster Penitentiary:**

Distorted, Volume 1 (MM, prisoner/prison guard, dub-con, mindf*ck)
Audio available now!
Joyless, Volume 2 (MMF, prison guards, bi-awakening, second chance, kinky)
Brainwashed, Volume 3 (MM, doctor/patient, true crime)
Fragments, Volume 4 (MM, frenemies to lovers, jealous/possessive/pining)
Audio coming soon!
Shadowman, Volume 5 (MM, bi-awakening) – Coming in 2024-2025!
Ivory, Volume 6 (The Finale)
Alabaster Pen is available in audio!

The Control Room, a FREE Alabaster Pen short!

**Twisted Tales Collection:**

Serpent In White (MMM, dark romance, drug cult, age gap, foster brothers, retelling of the Brothers Grimm's *The White Snake*)

Standalone Novella:
Unwrap Him by Nyla K (An Age Gap, Taboo MM) – Available across all digital retailers, and Nyla's website!

Join my Facebook reader group for discussions, giveaways, and all the best Nyla K madness!

Don't forget to share and leave a review! It means the world!

About Nyla K.

Hi, guys! I'm Nyla K... Author of Flipping Hot Fiction, which basically means all things unique & boundary-pushing! If you're looking for the same old story, you won't find it here. I'm the... *bad guy* ;)

I'm an awkward sailor-mouthed lover of all things romance, existing up in Maine—in our dream house in the woods—with my partner, who you can call PB, or Patty Banga if you're nasty, and our fur baby, Ziggy Stardust! When I'm not writing and reading sexy books, I'm rocking out to <u>my various awesome playlists</u>, cooking yummy food and fussing over my kitten (and no, that's not a euphemism). Did I mention I have a dirtier mind than probably everyone you know?

I like to admire hot guys (don't we all?) and book boyfriends, cake and ice cream are my kryptonite. I can recite every word that was ever uttered on *Friends*, *Family Guy*, and *How I Met Your Mother*, red Gatorade is my lifeblood, and I love to sing, although I've been told I do it in a Cher voice for some reason. I'm very passionate about the things that matter to me, and art is probably the biggest one. If you tell me you like my books, I'll give you whatever you want. I consider my readers are my friends, and I welcome anyone to find me on social media any time you want to talk books or sexy dudes!

Get at me:

info@authornylak.com
Visit AuthorNylaK.com for Signed Books & Merch!

The Flipping Hot Newsletter!:
https://view.flodesk.com/pages/60c62e5858d33ffd60199e7e

Patreon: Nyla K
Where you'll find Nyla K UNCENSORED!

Instagram:@AuthorNylaK

Facebook: AuthorNylaK

Tiktok: @NylaKAuthor

Twitter: @MissNylah
(Misc uncensored content! NSFW!)

Goodreads: Nyla K

BookBub: @AuthorNylaK

Happy reading!

Made in the USA
Coppell, TX
17 December 2024

42867740R00125